3 8002 01206 3808

'You make me want to slap you!'
Abby said in

COVEN

D0717106

Please return this book on or before the last
date stamped below.

To renew this book take it to any of
the City Libraries
before the date
due for return

Coventry City Council

Cathy Williams is originally from Trinidad but has lived in England for a number of years. She currently has a house in Warwickshire, which she shares with her husband Richard, her three daughters, Charlotte, Olivia and Emma, and their pet cat Salem. She adores writing romantic fiction and would love one of her girls to become a writer—although at the moment she is happy enough if they do their homework and agree not to bicker with one another.

THE GREEK'S FORBIDDEN BRIDE

BY
CATHY WILLIAMS

All the characters in this book have no existence outside the imagination of the author, and have no relation whatsoever to anyone bearing the same name or names. They are not even distantly inspired by any individual known or unknown to the author, and all the incidents are pure invention.

All Rights Reserved including the right of reproduction in whole or in part in any form. This edition is published by arrangement with Harlequin Enterprises II B.V. The text of this publication or any part thereof may not be reproduced or transmitted in any form or by any means, electronic or mechanical, including photocopying, recording, storage in an information retrieval system, or otherwise, without the written permission of the publisher.

This book is sold subject to the condition that it shall not, by way of trade or otherwise, be lent, resold, hired out or otherwise circulated without the prior consent of the publisher in any form of binding or cover other than that in which it is published and without a similar condition including this condition being imposed on the subsequent purchaser.

MILLS & BOON and MILLS & BOON with the Rose Device are registered trademarks of the publisher.

First published in Great Britain 2005
Harlequin Mills & Boon Limited,
Eton House, 18-24 Paradise Road, Richmond, Surrey TW9 1SR

© Cathy Williams 2005

ISBN 0 263 84162 6

Set in Times Roman 10½ on 12 pt.
01-0705-52447

Printed and bound in Spain
by Litografia Rosés, S.A., Barcelona

CHAPTER ONE

FROM the sprawling veranda outside his bedroom Theo Toyas had a clear and unimpeded view of the drive leading up to his grandfather's fabulous villa. It was six-thirty in the afternoon, and the ferocious heat of the day was beginning to give way to something a little more acceptable. Even so, it was still too hot for anything other than a pair of light chinos and a short-sleeved shirt.

In one hand he nursed a whisky on the rocks, which he had been periodically sipping for the past half-hour, content to just sit back on the cushioned wicker lounging chair and watch the scenery. And the scenery was indeed magnificent. To the right, just a short walk from his bedroom, was a stunning infinity pool overlooking Santorini's famous flooded volcano. Meticulously manicured gardens swept around the pool and curved towards the drive, which had been impressively designed to give the illusion of dropping off the side of the caldera.

He had forgotten how tranquil and soporific the place was, but then again he rarely visited the villa. In fact, appreciating scenery was something Theo didn't do much of. He simply didn't have the time. He lived his life between London, Athens and New York, controlling the vast shipping empire which his great-grandfather had founded and which was now his legacy. Taking time out was almost unthinkable.

But then an eightieth birthday was not something that came around often and his grandfather's eightieth, to be celebrated in the villa on the very island where he had met his wife, was the equivalent of a royal summons. Most of the family members who lived on mainland Greece would be there for just the party, flying in on private planes which had been chartered for the purpose. Others, from as far afield as Canada, would be staying for the full week at the villa, or else hiving off to stay with other family members in other parts of Greece, some of whom they had not seen for a very long time.

Theo planned to stay for three days only, long enough to pay his respects and toast his grandfather's health before resuming his ferociously work fuelled life in London.

A taxi had stopped on the drive and he watched through narrowed eyes as first Michael, his brother, emerged from the car and then his companion.

So this was it. He was finally going to see this mysterious woman who had suddenly appeared on the scene. It had come as a source of relief to everyone, not least his mother and his grandfather. Theo might be single, yes, but he ostensibly enjoyed the company of women. He was also a pragmatist and fully comprehended the advantages of marrying the right girl with the right connections. He would, he had once dryly told them both, be married by forty. In the meantime, they were not to interfere with his private life.

Michael had always been another kettle of fish. Five years younger, he had always been a fragile child, prone to bouts of ill health. Whereas Theo had been sent to boarding school in England from the age of thirteen, something that had gone some way to giving him the hard-edged independence that had become the cornerstone of his formidable personality, Michael had been kept at home. Lina Toyas had not been able to face sending her delicate, sensitive son away from her. She had always worried about him and she still did. The fact that he had never brought home any nice girls to meet her had been just one more thing to worry about. He was shy, she knew, and shy men could often become lonely bachelors and that, for her, would have been a fate worse than death.

The sudden appearance of a girlfriend had brought tears of joy to Lina's eyes.

Theo, in receipt of this emotional telephone call, had been less thrilled.

Things didn't add up and he knew, as a shrewd businessman, that if something didn't add up then it was most probably wrong.

How was it that the name Abigail Clinton had never once crossed his brother's lips? Surely if they had been an item he would have mentioned her somewhere along the line, in one of the many calls he made to his mother in Greece from his home in Brighton? In fact, the girl's name had only been uttered a fortnight ago, when he had amazingly announced that he was engaged to an English girl and would be bringing her to his grandfather's birthday celebrations in Santorini.

Theo had tactfully refrained from voicing any of his suspicions to his mother. He intended to use his brief stay at the villa constructively. He would watch, question and determine whether the girl was, as he suspected, after his brother's money. Because Michael lived in Brighton and ran a couple of restaurants and a nightclub did not mean that he was unaffected by the fabulous Toyas wealth. In fact, he owned a great deal of highly valuable shares in the company and the trust fund into which he occasionally dipped was well beyond most people's wildest dreams. He lived a modest enough lifestyle, and at first glance might just come across as being an up-and-coming successful young businessman. That, as Theo knew only too well, was only the tip of the iceberg, just his brother modestly disassociating himself from the vast fortune that was attached to his name. Anyone interested in tapping into the mother lode would only have to do some rudimentary detective work and he was pretty sure that was exactly what had happened.

He was equally sure that he would do anything in his power to prevent his brother being exploited. Although he worried less about Michael than his mother did, he was still very protective of him. Michael trusted people, a huge drawback in life as far as Theo was concerned. To trust was to be vulnerable. Only fools were vulnerable.

He sat forward, black eyes hard as he focused on the girl emerging from the taxi. She was slight in stature, with long, very blonde hair, almost white-blonde in fact, which fell down her back in one perfectly satin-smooth, straight curtain. She kept playing with it, lifting it with one hand into a makeshift ponytail and then letting it drop, and all the while she stared around her, lips parted, taking in the opulence of the surroundings.

Clocking the price tag around Michael's neck, Theo thought cynically to himself.

Still, he conceded grudgingly, the boy had taste. He couldn't see the details of the girl's face but she was neatly built with slim legs and very slender arms. A boyish figure, barely filling the short, strappy dress. Unlike him, Michael had never shown the least interest in the voluptuous, sexy girls that Greece boasted.

He watched as suitcases were taken out of the taxi, his mind ticking along its ruthlessly logical path. When they disappeared from view he pushed himself off the lounger and sauntered into his bedroom, draining the remainder of the whisky in one gulp and dumping the empty glass on the sideboard in the room.

His room was typical of most of the many rooms in the enormous villa. It was luxuriously but simply furnished. The stained wooden floor was dominated by a large, brightly patterned rug and the walls were painted a pale terracotta, an effective backdrop for the cream curtains that hung from floor to ceiling. Against one wall was an impressive Syrian chest embellished with mother-of-pearl and above that hung a darkly compelling painting of the island's famous volcano by twilight. The majority of the furniture was of dark wood, which gave the room a decadent, opulent feel.

Theo barely noticed any of it. He was busy thinking, working out the best way to approach the girl without rousing his brother's suspicions or incurring his mother's displeasure. The latter, he thought to himself, would be slightly more of a challenge.

And who, he thought with a small smile, ever said that Theo Toyas didn't appreciate a challenge?

He was still contemplating the technicalities of revealing this gold-digger in their midst when, an hour later, he made his way to one of the sitting areas where he knew drinks would already be underway for the guests who had arrived. Not that many of them had so far. Most would be descending the following day, but on this first night there would essentially be just close family members. His grandfather, of course, and his mother, as well as uncles and aunts and their various offspring. And Michael and the woman.

Drinks were being served in the sitting area which overlooked the back gardens. He had spent a couple of pleasantly invigorating hours here earlier on with his mother, arguing the practicality of lighting up the outside area with lanterns and had, as he had expected, lost the debate. As he entered the sitting area, though, he had to admit that the effect was stunning.

The gardens seemed alive with giant fireflies and several of the guests were outside having their drinks, seduced by the romance of the scenery.

'I admit it looks rather splendid,' Theo said, grabbing a drink *en route* and strolling up to where his mother was quietly contemplating the stage she had masterfully set.

Lina turned to her eldest son and smiled. 'George likes it too. He fussed and fretted about all the effort involved, but look at him out there, puffing and preening like a peacock and accepting all the compliments. It is just a shame that your father is no longer around. He would have enjoyed the moment.'

Theo slung his arm around his mother's shoulder and nodded. 'We haven't had one of these family gatherings since…since that wedding five years ago. Elena and Stefano.'

'They will be here tomorrow. Along with their two children.' Lina turned to him and gave him a long, critical look. She was, he freely admitted, the only human being on the face of the earth who could look at him like that and get away with it. 'It could have been you,' she pointed out, without bothering to beat about the bush. 'You are not a young boy any longer. This dynasty needs its heirs, Theo.'

'And they will be produced,' Theo murmured placatingly, 'all in good time.'

'Alexis Papaeliou will be coming,' Lina ventured. 'She would be a good match, Theo. Her grandfather grew up with George. They still keep in touch now, even though it is not as easy as it once was.'

'Papaeliou…yes the name rings a bell. Alexis, pretty

name, and I have to admit that three months of celibacy is beginning to get to me.' He grinned as his mother blushed furiously at his outrageously personal observation, and then indulged her as she reminded him that he was bordering on being disrespectful. Her voice was teasingly indulgent, however, as he had known it would be.

'Of course,' he said lightly, looking out to the gardens and the clusters of chattering people with drinks in their hands, 'there is no rush for me now, is there? With Michael having won the race to secure a bride...'

'Now, Theo...'

'I am merely making an observation, dearest Mama...'

'In a tone of voice which I am not sure I like. I have met the young woman and she seems perfectly friendly, if a little dazed at the surroundings.'

I'll just bet, Theo thought to himself. The dazedness, he reckoned, would last just about as long as it took her to add up the millions looming just over the horizon. He opened his mouth to share some of these thoughts with his mother, and then thought better of it. She often accused him of cynicism and she would have a very good reason for doing so again now, although he preferred to use the term cautious.

'Where are they?' he asked casually.

'They'll be down in a short while,' Lina said. 'And Theo...be good.'

'Mama, I am always good.' He looked down at her and smiled as she shook her head and sighed. 'Michael loves this woman. I can see that. Do not spoil anything...'

'I'll bear that in mind,' Theo said noncommittally, and before he could be boxed into a corner, making promises he had no intention of keeping, he moved away, tugging his mother with him so that he could mingle with the guests.

But he was watching the French doors, all eight of them, which were thrown open to accommodate the easy flux of the guests as they went inside to sit, before strolling back out, drawn by the warmth and the seductive glow of the lanterns. His mind was half on the conversation he was having when they arrived. As soon as she saw the scene outside her hand flew to Michael's arm and he clasped it with his own, a gesture of reassurance. Theo watched as she looked up at Michael and said something and his brother smiled down at her, clearly urging her not to feel intimidated.

A charming charade, he thought. Was it for the benefit of his brother or for the congregation of people, who were now glancing over with interest in their direction?

Her outfit was certainly designed to impress the guests with her innocence. The pale dress was a testament to modesty. The neckline was rounded and buttoned to the top and although it did hug her top half the bottom swung in a swirl around her to her knees. And it was pink, the lightest of pinks, a colour associated with children. There she stood, hesitant and nervous and looking like the innocent he would have bet his bottom dollar she wasn't. The white-blonde hair was tied back in a neat braid, leaving her smooth, vulnerable neck exposed. In fact, he thought, that was precisely what she looked. Vulnerable. He gritted his teeth together impatiently and headed towards them, altering his expression as he approached and going through the genuine motions of greeting his brother before turning to her.

'My fiancée,' Michael said, grinning, 'Abby. Although I expect you have probably heard. News,' he said, turning to Abby, 'travels through this family at the speed of sound.'

Abby smiled and tried very hard to ignore the presence of the man standing next to Michael. He spoke a lot about his brother, Theo, whom he obviously admired, and in her head she had conjured up an image of someone not unlike Michael. Gentle, thoughtful, with the same teasing humour that had made her warm to him instantly.

She couldn't have been further from the truth.

There was nothing gentle about this man, although he was chatting easily enough with them. Even in the looks department he had somehow managed to take the dark good looks that Michael possessed and push them to the outer limits. His black hair was longer than his brother's, curling into the nape of his neck, and his eyes were like flint. Even his features were somehow harder and more ruthlessly defined. It all added up to a package that was intimidating, that sent little cold shivers of fear racing up and down her spine, although she had no idea why she should be afraid.

He was talking to her now, asking her something about the weather in Brighton, a perfectly harmless question, but when Abby looked at him she had the unnerving impression that something dark and threatening was stirring just below the surface.

She also found that her eyes were riveted to his face, which was compelling and scary at the same time.

She edged closer to Michael and knew that Theo had noticed that small shift in her stance, although his face remained impassively polite, his head tilted to one side with every semblance of hanging on to what she was going to say.

The man exuded power and menace. She heard herself stammering out some nonsense about winter by the coast,

followed by another humdrum remark about the lovely
weather here, how super it was to actually be able to
stand outside in the evening. In the middle of her tortured
reply Michael removed himself so that he could see his
mother and fetch them both a drink, leaving her floundering in sudden, inexplicable panic.

'You can't be that warm,' Theo drawled. He, too,
shifted his stance, although it was to block her off from
the guests behind him. In a minute he knew that his
mother would descend upon them and he intended to let
no part of his time be wasted. 'You're trembling.'

'Oh, I'm just…a little nervous, I suppose.' Abby
looked away. 'All these people…'

'Surely you are not nervous of mixing with our family.
They are a perfectly ordinary bunch.' He didn't smile
when he said this. He just kept looking at her in that way
that made her wonder what was going through his head.
'Although I can understand that tackling Michael on his
own might be a little different to dealing with…the rest
of us.'

'What do you mean by *tackling*?' Abby asked sharply.

'Why don't you come and meet the rest of the clan?'
Theo placed a hand on her arm to usher her in the direction of the assorted guests and he felt her instinctive urge
to pull away.

Not, he thought grimly, the sign of someone madly in
love with his brother and with nothing to hide. With easy
aplomb he directed her to his mother, taking time out to
observe her reactions, and then he continued to watch her
throughout the rest of the evening. His brother was as
solicitous as he had expected and away from *him* she
seemed to relax.

But then no one else was questioning her presence on
the island and in his brother's life.

Supper was served in the dining room, which had been built for entertaining. The table could seat twenty comfortably and Theo made sure that he nabbed a chair directly facing her, a position from which he could make his presence felt without being obvious about it. As was usual at these family affairs, the drink flowed and the conversation became more rowdy as the evening wore on. His grandfather, he was pleased to see, was in his element. Eighty, he exclaimed at one point during the evening, somewhere between the main course and the coffee, was just another two digit number!

By the time the liqueurs had arrived some of the guests had drifted off to bed, including his mother. The remainder were finding excuses to raise their glasses and toast anything and everything. When there was a lull in the raucous conversation, Theo banged his spoon on the table and waited until all heads had swivelled in his direction.

Abby, he noticed, was more cautious than expectant. Was she wondering what he was going to say? Her eyes were certainly watchful. And beautiful eyes she had too. Eyes designed to trap a man, or at least a man who had no great experience of the opposite sex. Brown, widely spaced eyes that he reckoned could turn sultry without too much difficulty. He raised his glass directly at her and drawled, 'To the beautiful Abigail Clinton on her engagement to my brother!' There was a roar of agreement and then he added softly, looking directly at her, 'Speedy though that engagement might be…'

Abby met his eyes and shivered. In the subdued candlelight his dark, handsome face looked almost devilish, but she raised her glass anyway, tilting her chin defiantly at him.

'Why waste time when two people know what they want?' she returned recklessly. With everyone else chatting loudly the conversation had a whispered, electric undercurrent that made her feel as though they were talking somewhere very intimate and very much alone. She resisted the uneasy feeling inside her and shot him a wide, bland smile.

She had hoped to disconcert him but he simply raised his glass to her in a silent toast and gulped down a mouthful, staring at her over the rim of the glass until her nerves got the better of her and she broke the eye contact, desperately searching out Michael, who was oblivious to any undercurrents and was busily telling one of the uncles about his latest venture into night life. She had to cough very loudly to get his attention, but when she finally did she was mightily relieved to see him immediately and unsteadily get to his feet and loudly bid good night to everyone at the table. He held his hand out for her and she practically rushed to take it, making sure not to actually meet Theo's darkly disturbing gaze as she hurried out of the room.

She only breathed a sigh of relief when they were in their bedroom and the door was firmly locked behind them.

'So,' Michael said, 'what do you think of my family?'

'Very…lively.' She smiled back at him and went over to the dressing table where she began untying her long hair, running her fingers through the braid to separate the strands of flaxen blonde. 'Your mother's wonderful, so friendly. I'm not sure what I expected. Mothers can be a little possessive when it comes to their sons.' Their eyes met in the mirror and he grinned at her.

'Ah, but I am not the first born, thank Heavens. The heaviest expectations are on Theo's shoulders. Not that he doesn't live up to them.'

'You do too, Michael.'

'Hardly.' The smile dropped for a minute but then he relaxed and moved behind her, massaging her shoulders until some of the tension eased away from her. 'You can see why it helps so much that I have brought you along...Abby, you're the only person I trust and I can't tell you how much it means to me...'

'Don't say it.' She swung around to face him and pulled him down so that he was kneeling in front of her. 'I trust you too...we're good for each other, Michael. It cuts *both* ways. I only hope...'

'What?'

'Your brother doesn't seem to like me,' Abby said bluntly. 'Did you notice? I got the feeling that he was looking at me, I mean *really looking at me*. When everyone was at the table and he offered that toast to our engagement, he just leaned towards me after everyone else had carried on talking and said something about it being a *very speedy* engagement.'

'Don't worry about Theo,' Michael said reassuringly. 'He's just an older brother. He's always been like that. We didn't go to the same schools. He went to England to board, but I can remember him coming back for holidays and he would always be there, at my school gates, making sure that everything was all right.' A smile of affection lit up Michael's attractive face. 'He knew about me being bullied, you see. I didn't want Mum involved, but Theo wasn't standing for any of it. He only had to show up a couple of times, and it never happened again. He is like that, Abby. Always there for the family.'

'Yes, but...'

'But nothing. Do not worry.' He stroked her arm fondly. 'He will be able to see that we are very happy in each other's company and that will be enough.'

Abby wasn't too sure. Two hours later her mind was

still worryingly focused on Theo, on that dark, sexy face staring at her, considering her, trying to get inside her head.

In the opaque darkness she could make out Michael's shape on the long, elegant sofa by the window, could see his chest gently rising and falling. Michael would never see the darkness behind the light, he was just that sort of person, but she could see it. Theo Toyas unsettled her. There was a still watchfulness about him that had made the hairs on the back of her neck stand on end, and even now, in the sanctuary of their room, she could still feel that shiver of apprehension just thinking about him.

Things didn't seem so bad in the morning.

She woke early, missing the comforts of her own place and missing her son. Michael was still sleeping and she smiled fondly at the figure curled under the blanket. He could have shared her bed, he knew that, but he had chosen the sofa and she had been quietly relieved. The only body she was accustomed to sharing her space with was that of a five year old, and it would have been uncomfortable having Michael in bed with her, even though he would have kept to his side. He was not a restless sleeper.

Abby clambered out of bed. Dozing had become a thing of the past. Ever since she had had Jamie her body clock seemed to have been reset to waking up early and collapsing in bed by ten.

She tiptoed across to Michael and gently shook him until he had surfaced into a state of groggy wakefulness.

'I need to phone Rebecca and speak to Jamie,' she whispered, stroking back his hair, which was sticking up in odd directions. 'Where's the phone in this place? I don't want to burst into anyone's bedroom but I might as well call now while everyone's still asleep.'

'Out of the bedroom…hmm…' He half sat up and frowned. 'God, it's been so long since I've been here… Why don't you use my mobile instead? You can go down to the pool and call. Out through the front door and then turn right and keep going. Want me to come with you?'

'And deprive you of your beauty sleep?' Abby grinned. 'Wouldn't dream of it.' She spent a scant fifteen minutes washing her face and brushing her hair, then she changed into a pair of cropped jeans and a T-shirt and headed out with Michael's phone.

This was the first time she had been away from her son and she was missing him as much as she had known she would, even though she knew that he would be fine back in England. He was at school during the day and he adored Rebecca, who had moved in for the duration of the week to look after him.

She was already dialling the number as she made her way outside to the pool area, which was a way away from the front of the house and surrounded by protective foliage. She glanced up once and almost faltered at the beauty of the spot.

Although the gardens were lush, the natural glory of the caldera was in its rocky magnificence, sloping downwards to the still, flat water of the volcano.

She could admire later, she thought, turning her back on both the pool and the view and finding a little spot of privacy on a chair by the side. Right now she needed to get through to her son before he headed off to school.

His voice, when she finally heard it down the end of the line, after a few minutes of chatting to Rebecca, brought an instant smile to her lips. She drew her legs up and leaned back, eyes closed so that she could picture his little face, her long hair tumbling over the back of the chair.

He had a secret. He wasn't supposed to tell. It took all of ten seconds for him to gleefully inform her that Rebecca had tucked a chocolate bar into his lunch-box. But there was some fruit too, he hastened to assure her. He babbled on, with Abby interjecting here and there, content just to listen to his childish ramblings. In her mind, she could picture him with his toffee-coloured hair rumpled, dwarfed in his uniform, which she had sensibly bought one size up so that it could last a bit longer. His thin legs would be dangling from the kitchen stool and his grey socks would be pushed down because all the other boys wore theirs like that.

'I'll call again later,' she promised, hearing the catch in her voice and taking a deep breath to steady herself. 'Don't forget to draw me a picture for when I get back. We can put it up on the notice-board next to the one of the dinosaur.'

From the veranda Theo watched silently as the telephone call was ended and she remained where she was, her face soft, lost in her own private thoughts.

His mouth tightened as he considered her. There was only one thing that could make a woman look like that and it was a man. And there was only one reason why she would have slunk out of the house at the ridiculously early hour of six-thirty to make a call, and it was because she couldn't afford to make the call in front of Michael.

With the fluid, soundless movements of a panther, he fetched his towel from the bathroom and took the round-about route to the pool.

Abby, still pleasantly absorbed in thinking about Jamie, was unaware of anyone approaching until he spoke and then she jumped, spinning around in shock.

'I'm sorry,' she stammered, half rising as he emerged to stand in front of her. 'I didn't hear you coming.'

She felt her skin start to prickle with a mixture of fear and awareness as she took him in.

The full force of his male beauty hit her like a sledgehammer. He was more bronzed than his brother and vibrated with a powerful masculine attraction that Michael somehow lacked. The light of day did nothing to diminish the impression. If anything, he seemed more imposing with the harsh early sun accentuating his strong, hard features and those cold, fathomless eyes that were now boring into her with as little warmth as they had done the night before.

'I have never developed the habit of sleeping in,' Theo drawled, 'even when I am taking time off work. And neither, I gather, have you. I could not help but notice that you were making a phone call.'

'You mean you were spying on me?' Abby asked, wondering wildly how long he had been standing behind her before making his presence known. Had he overheard her conversation? She and Michael had agreed that they wouldn't mention Jamie just yet. One step at a time, he had said, and step one would be to introduce her to his family.

For different reasons, Abby knew that it would be a huge mistake to breathe a word about her son to the man carefully and insolently looking down at her.

'Now I find that a very odd remark,' Theo said speculatively. She had looked young and vulnerable last night, in her baby-pink dress, and she still looked young and vulnerable now, even though she was in figure-hugging faded cropped jeans and a T-shirt that barely skimmed her top half, leaving a slither of flat stomach visible. Her hair, he could now see, was a streaky blonde colour, the sort that most women would pay to attain, though he doubted she had been one of them. Young, vulnerable and one hundred per cent natural. Vital ingredients when it came to trapping a man, because what man could resist the charm of the untouched?

'Why do you imagine that I would be spying on you?' he asked. 'Surely that would imply that I might think you have something to hide. And you haven't, have you…?'

Abby felt telltale colour spread slowly across her cheeks. She was sitting bolt upright; their eyes locked together and she opened her mouth to laugh off his remark but nothing emerged for what seemed like the longest time.

Something to hide. Where to begin? she could have asked. The thought that he might find out anything at all made her skin crawl.

'I should be going back in,' she finally said, standing up on trembling legs.

'Why? No one will get up for at least another hour or so. I'm about to have a swim. Why don't you join me?' Theo could have kicked himself. The first rule of making the kill was to avoid scaring off the prey. So what did he do? Jump right in and start with the accusations.

'Join you?' Abby asked, aghast. 'No, really, it's very kind of you to offer but I'll leave you in peace…' She took a couple of steps backwards, and then he smiled. It was a smile of such devastating charm that it almost knocked her sideways.

'I am a man who finds peace very hard to deal with,' he murmured persuasively. 'Is that very sad, do you think?'

'Yes, yes I do, actually,' Abby replied breathlessly, and he frowned.

'Why?'

'I've got to go.'

'You can't possibly. It would be cruel of you to call me sad and then run away without bothering to elaborate on it.'

'Oh, no, I didn't mean…what I *meant* was…'

'Go and get your swimsuit. We can finish this conversation in the pool. Or perhaps you would be happier just to sit by the side of the pool while I swim? Hmm?'

'Yes! I mean…no!'

'Besides,' Theo said lazily, 'Michael would like us to get to know one another, I am sure. He and I may not have grown up together in the normal fashion, what with me being sent to board from thirteen, but we are still close. He would be appalled if he thought that I… intimidated you…'

CHAPTER TWO

OF COURSE, that was what did it.

The implication that he intimidated her, that she wanted to run away from him.

Abigail thought of herself as something of a fighter. She had brought up Jamie on her own, had gone through the entire pregnancy without the support of anyone, and had been almost mortally wounded by the spectacular collapse of her relationship with her son's father. She herself had no parents on whom to fall back and no handy network of caring relatives who could rush to her clarion call when she needed them. The only two weapons in her armoury had been her resolve to bring this baby into the world and her determination to give him all the love she was capable of giving.

To have Theo Toyas insinuate that she was running scared was like a red cloth to a bull.

Michael, as she expected, was soundly asleep when she quietly entered the bedroom to get her hat, her sun-cream and her book. The restaurant and nightclub business meant that he kept unsocial hours and could never resist the temptation to lie in whenever he could. She decided against breaking into his deep slumber for the second time to tell him where she was going, and instead headed back out towards the pool.

Just as Theo had predicted, no one was as yet up.

An hour ago it would have sent her into a tailspin to think that she was going to be alone with the man, who she was beginning to think of as a bully whatever

Michael had to say on the subject, but now she strode out with the bit very firmly between her teeth.

It was to find him already in the pool, cutting through the water with the fluidity of a fish. She watched for a few minutes, fascinated by the movement of muscle, and then slowly walked towards one of the sun loungers.

She tried to take in the breathtaking view, to relish the illusion of the pool leading straight out on to the horizon, but time and again she found herself staring at the body scything through the water until finally she stuck her hat on and relaxed back, linking her fingers lightly together.

This time she was aware of his approach even though her eyes were closed. She heard him emerge from the pool and then the slap of his feet as he dragged a chair over to her and sat down.

'I didn't think that you would take up my invitation to join me,' Theo said, looking down at her, at that slither of pale skin where her top ended and her jeans began. Her breasts were two small mounds pushing against the thin cotton of her T-shirt.

'Why shouldn't I? Besides, you're right; Michael would want us to be friends or at least to make an effort to be amicable.'

Women didn't usually view him as an object of dislike with whom effort was needed to be amicable but he let it go.

'Is this your first visit to Greece?' he asked instead, keeping his voice even. Her eyes were still closed and he found himself looking, unobserved, at those small, rounded breasts. A handful, no more. With some effort he looked away.

Abby opened her eyes and reluctantly looked at him. His hair was wet and slicked back and his body had that still damp sheen from the water. Frankly, she wished he would put his shirt back on because that hardened, well-muscled torso was just a little too much in her face for her liking.

'My first visit to Santorini,' Abby said coolly, averting her eyes and staring straight ahead, which was a far more calming view. 'I've been to Athens. A few years ago.'

'With your family?' Theo asked.

'No.'

Since she obviously didn't want to expand on her answer, he sat back and waited in silence. Sooner or later she would fill it. People were predictable. And, since he wanted to find out as much about her as he could in the limited time at his disposal, he would wait for her to supply the details that would eventually bury her.

'I don't have any family. At least not in England,' Abby eventually said irritably. 'My parents went to Australia to live seven years ago. We don't see one another very often, I'm afraid.'

'You went with friends, then?' Theo prompted. 'Athens is a beautiful city, but I'm surprised you would have chosen that as a destination with friends. It lacks the rampant night-life of some other places, like Ibiza. Isn't that where most young English people go to have a good time?'

'Most,' Abby agreed, resisting the bait. Athens was just one of those things she had no intention of talking about. Actually, even thinking about that long weekend there made her feel slightly sick. It had been the last time that she had known complete, innocent happiness. She had been in love, or so she had thought, and the world had been a very rosy place. Looking back on the person she had been then was like looking back at a stranger.

'So you don't know much about our island.' Theo could barely contain the impatience in his voice. 'Or do you? Did Michael tell you anything about it? I can't re-member the last time he was here.'

'Oh, no. He didn't discuss it much. Just said that the villa was your grandfather's holiday home and that he was having his birthday celebrations here.'

'And has the villa lived up to your expectations?' he enquired silkily.

Abby stiffened. 'I didn't really think what to expect.'

'Come now, surely that's not true. Everyone has a vi-sion in their mind when they're heading off somewhere on a holiday.' He omitted to mention the word *free* to describe her one week stay but it was on the tip of his tongue.

'It's a magnificent house,' Abby said neutrally. She turned towards him and gave him a long, cool look. 'Is that the right answer or is there something else I ought to say? I'm surprised by its size but only insofar as it seems big for one person to use as a holiday home.'

She might look like a girl of nineteen, he thought, but there was nothing infantile about her mind. Had he really expected that there would be? Any gold-digger worth her salt would have the shrewdness of a fox and would be clever enough to know how and when to use it. Of course she wouldn't have tried to squeeze too much information out of his brother about where they were going. That would lead to suspicions. Even his trusting brother would be wary of the third degree, no matter how skilfully han-dled.

'It was built at a time where there were far more family members around to use it. My grandmother was still alive and all their children were still at home. Then, for a short while, there were grandchildren. Times have changed but my grandfather's affection for the island is still the same and he still chooses to come here every so often so that he can appreciate the peace of the surroundings. Naturally, Santorini is far more touristy than it used to be, but he contents himself with staying in the house and has very little idea of the shops and boutiques and hotels that have gone up in the past couple of decades.'

'Doesn't he get lonely, coming here by himself to relax?' Abby was drawn into the conversation against her will. It was safe enough, she supposed, and besides, like it or not, he had a mesmerising voice, dark and deep like velvet.

'My mother accompanies him whenever she can and usually brings some of her friends.' Theo sat back in the chair and gazed out towards the endless landscape. 'My grandfather is old. It would be more stressful for him to start taking holidays in a hotel some place he didn't know than to come back to what he knows. Timos and Maria, who look after the place when it's empty, have been here for ever. They are almost as old as he is and they are as familiar with him as old friends. Often, if he is here by himself, he will share his meals with them.'

'And do *you* ever come here on holiday?' Abby asked curiously.

'I don't tend to have holidays,' Theo informed her flatly.

'Why not?'

'I beg your pardon?'

'Why don't you take holidays? Are you one of these people who thinks that relaxation is some kind of sin?'

Theo looked at her incredulously. The way she addressed the question was very nearly bordering on insolent. Insolence was not a quality he *ever* encountered, not in the people he met in the line of work and especially not in the women with whom he came into contact. And the way she was looking at him, big brown eyes wide and steady and ever so slightly disdainful, made his pulse accelerate with anger.

A gold-digger, he thought, a common little gold-digger daring to cross verbal swords with him!

'I run a vast and complex empire, Miss Clinton, and, crazy though this may seem, rushing off on holiday every two weeks is not a key ingredient to my success.'

'People always think they're indispensable but they never are. Michael often says that he may have opened two restaurants and a nightclub, and they may be doing well, but the most important role he could play would be to ensure that they carried on running well even if he wasn't around. A bit like having a child, I guess. You put everything into bringing them up and of course they need you, but in the end, if the parenting is halfway decent, they're confident enough to spread their wings and find their own destiny.'

'And what would you know about children?'

Abby could have kicked herself. Theo Toyas was dangerous. She should have had her guard up instead of finding herself lulled into meaningful conversation. 'I'm just saying that never looking up from the grindstone seems a pointless way of life.' She shrugged, which sent his anger levels rising. To top it off, she actually turned away from him, dismissing him from her line of vision so that she could stare out towards the horizon.

His plan to find out about her had well and truly backfired and if he wasn't so stunned he would have been substantially angrier with her.

He decided to postpone his inquisition for a little while longer. 'Naturally I have highly dependable and talented people but I control the reins of my organisation. Call it doing things *the Greek way*.' Her face, like her body, was neat. Small straight nose, sprinkling of freckles, surprisingly dark eyebrows for someone so blonde. He caught himself staring and gritted his teeth in exasperation.

'Okay.'

'Okay *what*?' Theo grated.

'Okay I'll call it doing things the Greek way if it makes you feel better.'

Theo controlled himself with difficulty. 'Tell me, how long have you known my brother?'

'Oh, a couple of years.'

'A couple of years. You've been going out with my brother for a couple of years and your name has only managed to surface now? I find that very hard to believe. Michael calls our mother every week. He would have talked about you a lot sooner.'

'I said that *I've known him for a couple of years*, and I have. We've been friends for a while.' Abby could feel herself slipping into dangerous territory. She knew where he was going. Thinking about it, she had seen the drift of his suspicious little mind the minute she had clapped eyes on him and she couldn't afford to antagonise him into digging any deeper. She had to convince him that everything was precisely as it seemed and getting under his skin was not the right way to set about the task.

She turned to face him and smiled. Warmly, she hoped. 'We clicked straight away. Michael's got all the qualities I admire in a man. He's kind and thoughtful and modest. You would think that in his line of work those are exactly the qualities that would let him down, but all his staff adore him and so do I.'

'And how did you two meet?' He could hear the sincerity in her voice but he couldn't abandon the suspicion that it was all a little too good to be true. People were never straightforward towards each other when it came to dealing with vast sums of money.

'I worked for him,' Abby said simply. 'I was the accounts manager for his restaurants when they opened up. At first there was just me and a secretary, but as they've become more and more successful the team has grown. Now, there are ten of us and we work flat out. You've never been to Brighton to see Michael, have you?'

'It is easier for my brother to travel to London to see me, usually for lunch, although lately we have not met as often as we might have hoped. We both have busy schedules.'

'His restaurants are super,' Abby enthused, eager to elaborate on a safe topic. 'One is a pub-style restaurant. Lovely cosy place but with superb French food, and the other's fancier, although the menu is really quite simple. We've found that most people don't actually want to go out and be faced with a choice of weird things. They like their food to be tasty and fairly straightforward, so we do fantastic sausages and garlic mash, and slow-cooked shin of beef and other dishes along those lines. It's very popular. In fact, at the moment there's a two month waiting list for tables at both restaurants.'

'What a charming eulogy to my brother's culinary ventures,' Theo drawled. 'I'm sure he would have found such enthusiasm very inspiring when he was first starting out.'

Abby tried not to show her intense dislike for the man sprawled in the chair next to her. Every inch of him spoke of arrogance. She had the unnerving sensation that he was circling her, taking his time, trying to find the chink in her storylines that would validate his low opinion.

'I hope so,' Abby said equably. 'It's a tough business

starting out on your own. Other people's support can be invaluable.'

'And is this when my brother began appreciating your *invaluable* contribution to his life?'

'Oh, I wasn't the only one who had confidence in his success.'

But I bet you were the only one who had the added advantage of some seriously persuasive feminine wiles, Theo thought. Abigail Clinton might not have the immediate, obvious sex appeal of the full-busted hourglass centrefold, but he had to admit that there was something alluring about her.

'You should get your swimsuit,' he said, changing the subject. 'The pool is lovely. Always at its best when no one else is in it.'

'I haven't brought one.'

'You *haven't brought one*?'

Abby blushed and looked away. 'I…I'm not that confident when it comes to swimming,' she confessed grudgingly. 'I did think about bringing one so that I could tan on a beach some time, but then I changed my mind.'

For the first time hostility and apprehension gave way to simple embarrassment and she felt her skin begin to tingle uncomfortably under his piercing black stare.

'It's not *that* unusual,' she snapped, scowling. 'Lots of people can't swim.' She turned a deeper shade of pink as a slow smile of amusement curved his lips. 'It's all right for you—' Abby flung herself into the ensuing silence, redolent with his silent laughter at her expense '—you grew up surrounded by swimming pools and sea! Some of us didn't!'

Theo was intrigued. He had wanted valuable information, information he could use to build up his case against her so that he could prevent a travesty of a marriage taking place, but this useless snippet was curiously engaging.

'I didn't think that you needed to be surrounded by swimming pools and sea in order to learn to swim,' he said, staring at her flushed face. 'I thought schools in England offered swimming lessons as part of the curriculum.'

'They probably do!' It was out before she had time to think. It wouldn't take a genius to work out the next logical question to her outburst and she waited in gloomy silence for the inevitable.

'You mean you didn't go to school in England? Did you grow up in Australia? Is that why your parents returned there?'

Abby looked at him with a hunted expression. 'No, I didn't grow up in Australia. I had an unusual upbringing,' she eventually muttered.

'How unusual?' He sat forward, resting his elbows on his knees, and continued to look at her with what she thought was an unhealthy level of interest.

Couldn't the man see that she was uncomfortable? Yes, she thought waspishly, of course he could, which would be no reason for him to back away from the subject. Well this, at least, was no great secret, was it?

'My parents were…a bit unorthodox. They travelled a lot.'

'You mean they were gypsies?'

'Of course they weren't gypsies! Not that I have anything against gypsies, as it happens! But do I look like a gypsy to you? Do I? With this hair?' She yanked off the hat and extended one long handful of her amazing hair towards him. Theo realised that he was thoroughly enjoying this surreal turn in the conversation. He took the proffered hair and made a show of examining it carefully.

'Could be dyed,' was his comment as she snatched it out of his fingers.

'I've never dyed my hair in my life.'

'So explain.'

'Okay. If you *really must know*, my parents were… were…sort of…hippyish.' There. It was out. She waited for the roar of laughter and the immediate attack. Instead he was looking at her with real interest. 'They didn't believe in material possessions or settling down. When I was older, Mum told me that life was one long adventure and what was adventurous about settling down with a mortgage and a job at the bank? So they travelled. Course, I did go to school but never anywhere for very long, not long enough to…'

'Take swimming lessons? Make friends?'

'Of course I made friends! Lots of them over the years.' But they had come and gone and her parents had never understood that whilst they saw that ever-changing parade of people entering and leaving her life as exciting, she found it very hard to deal with. She had never really even had the opportunity to have boyfriends in the normal way. What would have been the point? They would have been short-lived anyway. Which, with the benefit of hindsight, had made her a walking target for being hurt, because when her parents left for Australia and she could finally impose stability on her life, she just didn't have the accumulated experience to spot the cad. Oliver James had been charming and persistent and she had fallen for him hook, line and sinker, never spotting all the inaccuracies in his behaviour that most other girls would have seen a mile off.

That, she thought, was something Theo Toyas would never learn about!

'That was incredibly selfish of your parents. Why did they decide to go to Australia?'

'More space to wander.' Abby grinned sheepishly. 'Although they tell me that they've now opened a shop in Melbourne, selling organic food and ethnic ornaments. They've even bought themselves a small house and they're planning on coming to England next year for a three month holiday.'

'I'd like to meet them,' Theo surprised himself by saying. He was picturing her as a girl, trekking in the wake of her parents from one place to another, longing for stability so that she could be like everyone else.

Then he reminded himself that really this was just the sort of background that would encourage her to go after a man with money, a man who could promise her the security she craved.

'I don't often meet nomads in my day-to-day life,' he amended, backtracking on that fleeting impulse that had seen him wrapped up in her life story, hanging on like a kid listening to a riveting bedtime yarn. Touching though her little tale had been, it had nothing to do with the reality he needed to deal with. He gave her a brisk, cool smile and vaulted to his feet. 'I'm going to have one last swim before I go inside for breakfast. In case you don't know the routine, breakfast tends to be a buffet affair. Everyone's going to be busy getting ready for tonight, so I shouldn't expect to be waited on hand and foot if I were you.'

With that he turned his back and sauntered towards the pool, leaving her to simmer at the pointed dig in his remark. She was sorely tempted to throw her book at the back of that arrogant head of his, especially as it was a hardback, but no, giving in to emotion was a bad idea.

Instead she glowered and removed herself from the lounger and headed back towards the villa.

For a minute there she had very nearly forgotten how dislikeable he was and that wasn't going to do. For Michael's sake, she had to be on her guard.

The object of her protectiveness was still asleep and Abby nudged him with one finger until he rolled over and looked at her blearily. 'You can't spend all day in bed,' she informed him without preamble and Michael smiled at her drowsily.

'You sound like a wife.'

'Michael, be serious.'

'I *am* being serious.' He grinned. 'Where have you been, anyway?'

'By the pool.'

'You can't swim.'

'I *know* that, Michael. I was by the pool with your brother and I'm beginning to think that this engagement business wasn't a very good idea.'

That had him sitting up abruptly. Michael had a range of silk pyjamas. It was his only sartorial weakness. Today's number was a deep blue and beige Paisley. Abby fleetingly wondered whether his brother had a similar taste in pyjamas and concluded that the man probably didn't sleep in any at all. He didn't strike her as a pyjama-wearing type. She immediately squashed any follow-up to that line of thinking and focused on her partner, who was looking at her with a worried expression.

'Of course it's a good idea. You're not going to back out on me now, are you? Are you?'

'I just didn't think it through,' Abby mumbled. 'I can see why you wanted it, really I can, but now that I'm actually here, I don't like deceiving your mother. And your grandfather, for that matter. They're nice people.'

'We're not deceiving them,' Michael whispered urgently. 'And the reason we're doing this is *because* they're nice people. Please don't back out on me now, Abby. Please.'

'And another thing,' she said uneasily. 'Your brother suspects something.'

'What?'

'Well, for a start he thinks that I'm after your money.'

Michael grinned at that. 'Well, that's okay. He's way off target, then.'

'True, but the fact is that he's going to probe until he finds out the truth.'

'He's here for three days, Abs. How much probing can one man do in the space of three days?'

A normal man, she wanted to say, *not much, but your brother, more than I feel happy about.*

'I suppose I could just keep out of his way for the whole time,' Abby said, more to herself than to Michael. 'I mean, it shouldn't be too difficult. I can just stick to whoever happens to be around and make conversation.'

'Which would really make him think that you've got something to hide,' Michael mused with a frown. 'On the other hand, it might be better if you just try and convince him that he's wrong. I mean, talk to him, give him the impression that you and I adore one another. Which, incidentally, also wouldn't be a lie.' The boyish grin was infectious and Abby found herself reluctantly drawn into his optimism.

'And don't worry; we're only here for a week, then we'll be back in England and everything will return to normal once more. Look, I'll get dressed and we'll have breakfast and then what say we head down to the town and do a bit of touristy stuff?' He pulled back the covers, stood up and pulled her into his arms so that he could wrap her up in a big reassuring hug.

After the tension of being in Theo's company Abby gave in to the hug with relief. One of the most wonderful things about Michael was the friendship he so unstintingly gave her. She had agreed to the engagement because she loved him and she succumbed to the wonderful mixture of tenderness and affection that he inspired in her.

'But you just need to spend some time with him,' he said into her ear. 'Honestly, I know Theo can be a bit overwhelming but he has always been the fairest man I have ever known.'

'If he was that fair…'

'Fair but frighteningly old-fashioned in his beliefs. You have nothing to fear in his company. You're not after my money and we do care deeply for one another. So give me a few minutes and we'll head down for breakfast together. Okay?'

Half an hour later, they emerged to find that the household had finally awakened. From where he was sitting out on the front veranda, Theo watched as they joined in with the other guests, chatting and easy, their body language speaking of a certain closeness which he couldn't believe was all it was made out to be.

She had tied her hair back into two very loose plaits and it irked him to see how genuinely warm her expression was as she made conversation with the other relatives milling around the buffet, helping themselves to the warm breads and fruit and cheeses. She turned around to say something to Michael and his brother grinned at whatever she had said and bent towards her to murmur something. Some sweet nothing, Theo thought, watching the display through narrowed eyes. The poor fool. Take one sexy woman and one gullible man and you get a divorce within a year and a hefty settlement for a gold-digger.

He frowned. When had he stopped thinking of her as a girl with no figure to speak of and started thinking of her as a sexy woman?

The main thing, he mused to himself, still following them as they helped themselves to some breakfast and took their seats at the far end of the table with his mother and two uncles, was that he was there to look out for his brother. It was what families did. They protected one another at all costs.

As though suddenly aware of him staring at her, Abby lifted her eyes and stared across the room and out towards the veranda, to where he was sitting, watching them and sipping his coffee. Theo met her gaze with cool, speculative eyes and was quietly satisfied when she gritted her teeth together and hurriedly looked away. She might have taken his brother for a fool but he was damned if she was going to think that he was the same.

He drained his cup and sauntered back into the villa, pausing where the group was sitting and chatting and leaned on to the table, palms spread to support his massive body-weight.

'So,' he drawled, 'what are the plans for today?' He was addressing the group as a whole but his eyes were fixed on Abby, who ignored him by concentrating on her croissant.

His uncles and their wives were staying put, it seemed, so that the wives could help prepare for the party and begin receiving the flood of guests to the villa, while their husbands, in typical Greek fashion, relaxed by the pool and refrained from doing anything too active.

'We wouldn't want to get in the way, would we,

Nick?' Dimitri said in a self-sacrificing voice and, amid the laughter, Theo looked at his brother, eyebrows raised in a question.

'We're off to explore the town,' Abby inserted quickly. Five minutes ago, she had been relaxed. Now she felt as though a tiger had entered the flock of sheep and was prowling around with her set firmly in its sights. The minute she had spotted him over there, sitting outside with his coffee, she had known that he had been watching her. She should have smiled but had found that she couldn't. Those cool black eyes stripped her of all her normal reactions. She had had time to brace herself for him now, though, and she gave him a wide, bright smile.

'Michael's been telling me a few things about Santorini and I'm dying to have a look around. What about you? Will you be helping with the preparations or just relaxing?' Abby tried to imagine Theo Toyas helping with preparations but that was enough to stretch anyone's imagination. She doubted he knew how to chop an onion, never mind doing anything more elaborate, although, from what she had gathered, caterers were being flown in for the party and would pretty much be doing the lot without any intervention needed from anyone.

'We all want it to be just right,' Michael's mother had confided to her earlier. 'There will be his favourite foods. Everything will be perfect. I have even arranged for the flowers and napkins to be in his favourite colours. He is eighty and do not be fooled by his joviality. George has a heart problem and none of us knows whether this will be the last birthday he will be celebrating.'

This had not come as news to her. Michael had said very much the same thing himself before they left England. Reading between the lines, she realised that part of his urgency for this engagement was to produce the girlfriend his grandfather had always wished him to have, to at least let him see that his grandson now had the promise of stability within his reach.

'I have work to do.' Theo broke into her thoughts.

'Now that is a real shame,' Michael said, and they both looked at him. 'Darling, I know I promised to take you into Santorini, spend the day driving around and showing you the sights, but...'

In a split second Abby knew what was coming and she gave him as much of a warning glance as she could. He smiled blandly and ruefully at her and only flinched a little when she smartly jabbed him on his shin with her foot under the table.

'No matter, we can do it another time,' Abby said, knowing exactly what he had in mind and doing her best to avert that course of action.

'I *was* going to ask you if you could take my place, Theo. Abby's been really looking forward to our little excursion and I hate to disappoint her, but I had an email last night from my head chef in one of the restaurants, and there's some kind of problem with the seafood consignment.'

'Surely Tom can handle that at home,' Abby inserted grimly, which warranted another sad shake of the head.

'Would you believe that Tom's been struck down by a mystery bug?'

'Frankly, no. He's always been as healthy as a horse.'

Michael ignored the interjection. 'No matter if you have work to do, though, Theo. Perhaps you could take the car into town on your own, Abby, or would that be too boring? Actually, you could be driven in and then simply call when you want collecting. Bit disappointing having to do the tourist bit on your own, but...' He looked utterly crestfallen at this turn of events. 'Maybe I could grab an hour and meet you for lunch…no…best not to promise…you know how long these problems can take to sort out…'

'My work can wait,' Theo said decisively. It was obvious that the last thing Abby Clinton wanted to do was go anywhere with him, and he reasoned why. Too high a chance of being caught out in her little web of deceit.

Abby tried not to look appalled.

He stood up and for the first time Abby realised that, somewhere along the line, the rest of the guests had left the table. She had not even noticed their departure, so compelling had been Theo's hold over her and the invisible threat he promised. She had also been quite wrapped up in a natural urge to throttle Michael.

'It will be…delightful to show you around our little island…' He smiled and Abby gazed back at him with barely disguised horror. 'So why don't you meet me here in an hour's time?' Theo found himself enjoying the prospect of spending the day with his unwilling companion. His smile broadened considerably. He actually had work to do, but that could wait. He'd barely had the opportunity to get to know the girl, or rather to get her to know where he was coming from. Several hours on their own should do the trick…

CHAPTER THREE

THEO was waiting for her outside. Her heart plummeted like a stone when she spotted him standing in the drive by one of the cars, casually leaning against the bonnet with his back to her, speaking into a cellphone.

Her intention to strangle Michael had fizzled out at the first hurdle. He had smiled winningly at her and somehow managed to puncture her annoyance by pleading with her to be nice to his brother. It was the fastest way of squashing his suspicions, he had assured her. An open, friendly person, he had argued with that boyishly persuasive smile of his, was a person with nothing to hide, and his brother would quickly lose interest if he saw for himself that that was the case. Abby had reluctantly agreed but had felt constrained to remind him that he owed her big time.

Michael had always had the ability to get around her and she knew why. She trusted him. There was no dark, hidden agenda.

Still, standing here now and looking at Theo's broad back and lazy pose, she couldn't contain a certain amount of apprehension.

She had apologised profusely to Lina, in the hope that the older woman might see fit to consign her to party preparation duties, but no such luck. Instead she had smiled charmingly, promised longer conversations just as soon as all this hectic stuff was over and expressed delight that she was getting along so famously with Theo, who could be a handful.

He swung round to face her as soon as she began walking towards the car, snapping his cellphone shut and shoving it into his pocket.

He was wearing a pair of khaki coloured Bermuda-style shorts and a short-sleeved shirt which hung loosely over the waistband of the shorts. He looked cool, casual and very, very sophisticated, especially with the dark shades which shielded his eyes from her and made it virtually impossible for her to know what he was thinking.

'You really don't need to do this,' Abby announced flatly when she was within speaking distance of him. 'You have work to do and I'm more than happy to occupy myself by the pool or out in the garden with a book.'

Theo accepted her remark with a slight inclination of his head and, instead of answering, pulled open the passenger door of the car for her to get in.

'Not much of an adventure when you've been promised a sightseeing tour of the island, though, is it? Reading a book in a garden?' he murmured once inside the car. Behind the dark shades, she could only imagine the triumph in his eyes as he contemplated a morning of vicious cross-questioning.

'I didn't come here for adventures,' Abby said. 'I really didn't even expect that I would get much of a chance to explore the island. Michael said that once the party was out of the way, we would return at a later date and catch up on all the sightseeing we wouldn't be able to do this time round.' Faced with a day out in the hot sun, trailing along behind Theo and trying to deflect his arrows, Abby had changed out of her cropped jeans into something cooler—a short lime-green drawstring skirt that fitted on her hips and a small sleeveless white vest.

Now she felt hideously exposed even though she knew that Theo wasn't interested in looking at her legs.

'So what did Michael tell you about the island?'

'It's small and has some very good boutiques.'

Theo felt his mouth twitch. 'Remind me to tell him never to consider a job in the tourist industry. Okay, here are some facts. This island is one of the most violent volcanoes on the planet. Some think that three thousand years ago it wiped out the entire Minoan civilisation. And, believe it or not, there was no tourism to speak of until fairly recently, when people realised that add one famous crater to amazing black sand beaches and you get a must see resort.'

'And you don't approve?' Abby felt herself grudgingly drawn into the conversation. If her mission was to be super-friendly and allay any suspicions, then this was as good a place to start as any because she was genuinely interested in the history of the place.

'What small island really approves of tourism?' He glanced briefly at her and she wished again that he would remove the sunglasses.

'The ones that make a packet of money out of it?' Abby ventured.

'Doesn't mean that the natives like it,' Theo pointed out. He interrupted himself to point out various sights, drawing her attention to the colour of the rocks and the nature of the landscape, comparing it to other Greek islands. 'Of course,' he said, resuming his original topic, 'they all work towards promoting tourism because it involves promoting their own standard of living, but do you not agree that it deadens the authenticity of a place?'

'If I had the choice of a roof over my head and food in my stomach, and the price was to be polite to a few tourists for a few months of the year, then I know what I'd choose.'

'Ah, a practical woman.' *Or something else.* 'And here I was thinking that all women were romantics at heart.'

'Because someone is sensible doesn't mean that they're not romantic as well,' Abby said.

He wanted to dwell on the significance of what she had said, but decided to go down the tantalising route of finding out just a little bit more about her.

'I suppose wandering the land with your parents may have resulted in you not getting a large enough dose of reality to extinguish the notion of romance.'

Abby tore her eyes away from the impressive scenery to stare at him. *Remember you're being nice and friendly and open*, she thought. 'Maybe, although I must say I had a large dose of reality in the form of temporary housing and dodgy neighbourhoods. No, I tell a lie, we never really stayed anywhere dodgy. Wolf and River preferred villages to cities.'

'Wolf and River?'

Abby hadn't meant to say that. Not even Michael knew about those stupid names her parents had called themselves. Just uttering it out loud made her cringe with embarrassment. She stared resolutely ahead, chin tilted, and didn't say anything.

'Your parents were called *Wolf* and *River*?' Theo stole a glance at the stubborn profile. So she was a slightly more complex gold-digger. Probably why she had succeeded with Michael, who had never been one to fall for the obvious.

'They explained that they needed names to suit the people that they were. Course, I carried on calling them Mum and Dad.'

'Bet they loved that.'

'They accepted that I...wasn't like them. Anyway, that's all very boring. Tell me some more about the island. You said it's volcanic. Isn't that dangerous?'

Theo's eyes strayed fleetingly to her slender thighs, abundantly exposed thanks to the short skirt which had ridden up, and he tried to focus on the mission at hand.

'Did *you* have a nickname? Should I say a Freedom name?'

'Stream,' Abby said shortly. 'I made them promise never to call me that in public. You were telling me about the volcano danger?'

'I suppose it could have been a bit embarrassing in front of your peer group.'

Abby had a sudden memory of waiting to be collected by her parents and the tide of shame that had washed over her when they had arrived at the school gates and called her by their pet name. Her brief spell at that particular school had not been one of her happiest.

Even more amazingly, she was almost tempted to confess that little nondescript memory to the man sitting next to her. Fortunately she caught herself in time and instead made some innocuous remark about the island and was relieved when he picked up the thread of the conversation and began explaining to her about the place. The huge eruption that had occurred some three thousand six hundred years ago, he informed her, had produced tsunamis that had reached as far as Turkey. In the aftermath of that upheaval, new craters had been formed.

'They're sleeping,' he added. 'But under constant surveillance.'

'That's reassuring. Don't sleeping things have a nasty habit of getting up, though?'

'Hopefully not. Now, I'm going to take you on a ride.'

'What kind of ride?' Abby asked cautiously and he

turned to grin at her. His teeth looked amazingly white against the sleek bronze of his skin and she shivered at the sudden awareness she had of him, the kind of sexual awareness that a woman has for a man.

'A white knuckle one. Then we'll go and do a bit of shopping.'

The white knuckle ride turned out to be a breathtaking cable ride from the capital down to the old port. Abby found that she was clutching on to Theo as the cable car soared off the edge of the volcano, down past solidified lava flows and rock formations. She couldn't bring herself to look down at several points and turned her face into his shoulder, not at all caring that she could feel him shaking with laughter. By the time they made it down, she was virtually shaking.

'You sadist,' she said, stepping out on trembling legs.

'You coward,' he returned. His legs appeared perfectly firm.

'You could have warned me,' she muttered. 'And it's not funny.'

'No. And yes, I should have warned you.' It baffled him how someone as straightforward as she was, someone who was out to get hold of her brother's money, should also be so contradictory.

He wondered for the first time whether his judgement had been wrong. If so, it would be a first, but that didn't mean it was impossible.

'I promised you shopping,' he said, waiting for the inevitable refusal, which wasn't long in coming.

'I'm not much of a shopper.' Truth was, she wanted to buy a couple of things for Jamie, but that would have been out of the question with Theo guarding her side like a prison warder.

'In that case, you can window-shop and I'll do the shopping.'

Still feeling a little queasy from the hellish ride down, Abby couldn't resist an opportunity to snipe. Besides, why on earth should he have the monopoly on asking questions? Bit by bit he had managed to find out snippets of her past, without her realising, whilst she knew nothing about him aside from what his brother had mentioned to her over time. That he was older, highly successful, fair, protective and a lady-killer. He had also been to boarding school. That was the sum total of her insight into this man who was determined to cut her to shreds if he could.

'I didn't realise that business tycoons enjoyed shopping,' she needled. 'Isn't that a bit feminine?'

'Are you trying to tell me that I'm *feminine*?'

He sounded so deeply scathing that she decided to press her point a little further. 'There's nothing wrong with a man being sensitive. Or liking to shop, for that matter.' She had no idea where they were going next or even what direction they were walking in. She was fired up by the conversation and the chance to be the one in the driving seat for the first time. 'I guess some men need to know that they're wearing the best so that they can impress the opposite sex.'

'Perhaps some men do,' Theo agreed silkily, 'although I take it that you are not one of those women who is impressed by the cut of the cloth?'

'No.'

'So you would have still fallen in love with my brother if you had seen him in stained jeans and a sweater with holes?'

Fallen in love?

'I would love your brother whatever he wore,' Abby

said, sidestepping Theo's phraseology. 'Anyway, he wears jeans most of the time, really old faded ones, even if his jumpers don't have holes.'

'Maybe I should pay a little visit to Brighton and see for myself,' Theo mused aloud, and Abby felt tension claw in the pit of her stomach.

'He's very busy most of the time,' she said vaguely. Now they were taking a taxi somewhere, probably to these marvellous shops where he could splash his money around. Dressed down as he was, it was still glaringly obvious that his casual clothes had cost an arm and a leg.

Theo heard the evasiveness in her voice and pricked up his ears. 'Surely not too busy to see his only brother. Especially now that he is an engaged man. The more I think about it, the more I see that it would only be right if I were to personally come down and visit, take you both out somewhere to celebrate…'

'I thought that you spent most of your time in Athens,' Abby said faintly.

'Used to but that was quite some time ago. Before the company expanded the way it has. Now I spend a fair amount of time in London. I have an apartment in Knightsbridge.'

'We could come up and see you there,' Abby said eagerly. The thought of Theo Toyas finding himself in Brighton and then snooping around didn't bear thinking about. 'A much better idea, really. I know Michael really enjoys the city and, well, it would be nice for me to go as well. I don't often get to London.' Not with the constraints of being a single mum, she thought. Lord only knew what sinister connotation he would put on that particular fact. It would certainly all be grist to his mill, just another reason why she might want to target a rich man and get him to marry her. The best reason, in fact. And if he dug his heels in, then Michael, she knew, would crack. This whole charade was designed to let his grandfather be at peace in the knowledge that his favourite grandson was on the right road. If he ever found out... And the thought of his brother finding out, the brother he looked up to, his protector, terrified him.

Not for the first time, Abby heartily wished that she had never set foot on this perilous path. What did they say about first we practise to deceive...?

'Why don't you?'

'Why don't I what...?'

'Get to London. Surely my brother doesn't demand that you spend all your waking moments at his side?'

'No, of course not! I just...never seem to get around to it. You know how it is. You keep meaning to do things, go places, but then before you know it another year's gone and you haven't got around to doing either...'

'What things do you keep meaning to do?'

'What things do *you* keep meaning to do? There must be *something*. You can't be happy just working.'

'I don't just work,' Theo said lazily. He was leaning against the door of the taxi, his body inclined towards her, and he smiled slowly. 'I'm a great believer in playing as well.'

'Oh, are you?' Abby asked politely. 'And what sports do you play?'

Theo laughed softly and raised his eyebrows in amusement. 'The kind that involve willing members of the opposite sex.'

In the stretching silence Abby felt her face go redder and redder. She became aware of him watching her, amused by her agonised silence as she pictured just the sort of sport he had in mind.

'Of course, I play other sports as well.' He rescued her eventually but not until her body was burning with images she did not want to dwell on. 'Of a more conventional nature,' he carried on. 'I swim and I try and get to a gym at least once a week. It is not always easy. I have several bases around the world, but in my own way I am as much of a nomad as your parents were. Now, enough of me. It's time for us to do some shopping.'

Abby realised, in a daze, that they had returned to the capital. So much for sightseeing. Yes, she had seen some sights, but her head had been too wrapped up in her companion to really take them in. The camera she had tucked away in her handbag hadn't once been brought out.

'As capitals go,' Theo was telling her as he confidently strode along, 'this is not the most beautiful in the world, but there are some good designer shops.'

'I don't tend to buy designer clothes. I'd really much rather have a look at some craft shops. I wouldn't mind buying a couple of souvenirs to take home.'

'You said you didn't bring a swimsuit with you...'

'That's right.'

'Which is something that we are about to change...'

She realised belatedly that Theo had been striding along with a destination in mind, and the destination turned out to be a small swimsuit shop that reeked of expensive price tags and overzealous assistants.

Abby screeched to a halt and turned to him. 'I don't need a swimsuit.'

'Oh, but I think you do, simply because we're going to spend a couple of hours at the beach and it's highly impractical for anyone to go to a beach fully dressed.'

'I'm not going to a beach!'

'Why not? I told my brother that I would take you

sightseeing and beaches are all part and parcel of the tourist experience.'

'Michael wouldn't like it…'

'Why not?'

'Because…' She realised that they were blocking the door when a couple irritably weaved between them.

'Does he think that I might make a pass at his woman?'

'No, he does not! And that's extremely *rude*!'

Theo flung back his head and laughed. Then, when he had stopped laughing, he shook his head and stared down at her from behind his sunglasses. 'That's rich, coming from you.'

'By which you mean…?'

Instead of immediately answering, Theo moved her to one side, forcing her against the wall and then bending over her so that her nostrils were filled with his tangy masculine scent and her eyes had no room to manoeuvre around his powerful body. She felt as though she was choking in his presence.

'Why don't we stop playing games?' His voice was curiously non-aggressive and all the more chilling for that. He leaned into the wall, into *her*, blocking her completely on one side by resting his arm on the warm concrete by her head. 'We both know what this so-called engagement is all about. I watched you with my brother and I've waited for you to prove me wrong, but nothing you have done or said has managed to convince me that you are not after my brother for his money.'

'You're wrong,' Abby faltered, white-faced. 'How can you say that?'

'I can say that because I am not a gullible fool.'

'And Michael is?'

'Michael is…Michael. When most boys of fourteen

were discovering the joys of testosterone, my brother was thinking of new ways to marinade beef. There is a part of him that lives in his own little world and an even bigger part of him that trusts other people. He places little value on money and somehow expects that the rest of the world feels the same way. I know better.'

'You don't understand.' Abby felt as though she was drowning under a tide of misconceptions, none of which were in her power to put right.

'What don't I understand?' His cool voice pressed down on her like a physical force. It was all she could do to meet his eyes with some degree of control.

Her voice, however, wasn't being quite so co-operative. When she continued to look at him mutely, he shook his head in exasperation.

'Let's go get you a swimsuit. This conversation hasn't ended and conducting it here is not ideal.'

'You expect me to go to a beach with you *now*? After you've accused me...of...'

'We either have this conversation somewhere private or we have it back at the villa. Take your pick.'

'I'm not after your brother's money!' Abby pleaded one last time.

Theo's response was to spin round on his heel and head straight into the swimsuit shop and Abby had no option but to follow him. Conducting this inflammatory conversation at the villa, where they might be overheard by anyone at any time, did not even present itself as a possibility.

He was waiting for her in the middle of the shop, arms folded. One assistant was simpering next to him and on a chair by the cash register sat the other shop assistant, who was simpering from a distance. Theo was either oblivious to their fluttering eyelashes or else so used to women behaving that way around him that he had ceased to notice. He registered her entrance with a curt nod of his head and had only to look down in the direction of the assistant for her to leap into immediate action.

Abby had never been into a shop and received such suffocatingly subservient service.

'I don't want a swimsuit.'

The saleswoman smiled in the blank way of someone who hasn't quite understood and Theo launched into rapid Greek, the upshot of which was that half an hour later they emerged from the shop the better for a black bikini, which Abby was reluctantly wearing underneath her clothes.

They made the drive to the beach in silence, broken only by Theo informing her that there were towels in the trunk of the car as well as a hamper, which the housekeeper had produced at short notice.

He had obviously worked the whole day out, she thought. Butter her up with a few sights and some harmless conversation and then, when she began feeling safe, launch into his attack. He hadn't planned a speedy and polite sightseeing tour, he had earmarked the entire day because he wanted the time at his disposal to batter her defences.

Abby could feel her heart beating in trepidation as they drove along, finally arriving at what she was informed was one of the more popular beaches.

'The satellite islands are better for beaches,' he said, getting out of the car and stretching. 'But they are a ferry ride away.'

Abby didn't answer. Now that he had made clear his intentions, she just wanted the conversation to be over and done with, although she couldn't see a way out for her. Michael's theory of being nice hadn't worked.

Maybe his brother was right, maybe Michael was such a basically unsuspicious person that he couldn't understand how being nice to Theo was a waste of time and energy. Theo, with his arrogance and his thinly veiled threats, was in a league of his own.

He took the hamper down to the beach and managed to find a fairly secluded corner. Abby trailed along behind, glumly admiring the famous black sand, which really wasn't that black at all, and the calm, clear water which would probably be freezing.

'There is no need to look so depressed,' Theo said, once he had spread the towels, which were the size of double sheets. Beach towels meant for the beach, which involved one hundred per cent protection from any stray sand. He stripped off his shirt and she could see now that the shorts rode low on his lean hips, exposing the flat planes of his tautly muscled stomach.

'I'm not depressed,' Abby snapped. 'I'm angry that you've brought me here as a hostage so that I have no choice but to listen to you lay into me for things that just aren't true. I'm angry because you're treating Michael like an idiot who has to be supervised even when it comes to his love life! I don't know what you think you're going to achieve! Is your plan to just relentlessly batter away at me because you think I'll crack? You're arrogant and supercilious and quite honestly you don't deserve to have a brother like Michael who thinks the world of you!'

Theo's lips narrowed to a fine line. He could feel a thread of white anger spread through him as he took in her flushed face and her self-righteous stance, arms defiantly folded, body held in rigid, simmering tension as she glared at him. The foul-mouthed little gold-digger, he thought. That guileless act had taken his brother in and he had to admit that she had a way about her that seemed transparently vulnerable now and again… God, she had even got *him* curious about her at one point! But the mask was dropping, wasn't it? She was spitting fire now.

He ignored the outburst and stretched out on the towel, propping his head up on one of the extra towels he had brought.

'Well?' Abby demanded. 'Aren't you going to start?'

'Sit down and stop overreacting.'

'Overreacting!'

'Typical hysterical female behaviour.' He inclined his head and squinted up into the sun at her. Yes, if a bucket of freezing water was at hand, he was pretty sure he would now be the recipient of it.

'Typical hysterical female behaviour!'

'This conversation isn't going to progress very far if you repeat everything I say, is it? Now, sit!'

'You might think you own the world, *Mr Theo Toyas*, but you can't tell me what to do!'

'No, but I *can* point out that standing there in this heat is going to get pretty tiring in a minute and there's nowhere you can go. I have the keys to the car, not that you would have a clue how to get back to the villa anyway, and storming off to another spot on the beach will just result in you getting burnt to a crisp. This must be one of the only free shady areas not already taken up with people.' He turned away and waited and was gratified when she finally flounced down on the towel so that she could glare at him from a less elevated level.

'Well, get to the point then,' Abby snapped, 'but don't expect me to have any input because I won't.'

'When is the marriage set for?'

'I beg your pardon?'

'The wedding. Has a date been set?'

'No.'

'No? You surprise me. What's the point of an engagement if you're not going to get running up that aisle as quickly as possible?'

'Kind of blows a hole in your little theory, doesn't it?' Abby shot back with a little sneer. 'I guess you thought that I would have already bought myself a calculator so that I could start totting you the millions I was going to have at my disposal. Well, so sorry to disappoint but no date's been set and we haven't even talked about a wedding.' That was so utterly true that she couldn't prevent a certain amount of smugness from creeping into her voice.

'Why is that?' Theo asked, directing his question to the sky but then turning so that he could watch the expression on her face. Surprisingly, she had a very mobile face and he was an extremely astute watcher. People invariably gave away their true emotions and he could almost always spot it. It was a talent born from a lifetime's experience working in the cut-throat world of business where vast quantities of money regularly changed hands and where there were always people on the lookout for a short cut to some of that money.

He also had immense experience of women.

'What do you mean, *why is that*? Not every woman sees her life goal as getting a ring on her finger in the least possible time.'

'No, but most do and all would if they were given a huge financial reward waiting just round the corner.'

'Really? Then how is it that *you* never got married? I'm surprised some clever woman hasn't tried to make a beeline for this amazing Toyas wealth!'

'Oh, most have,' Theo remarked dryly. 'Needless to say, they get nowhere.'

'Poor Theo,' Abby mocked. 'Destined to be on his own for ever because he's convinced that the only reason a woman might go out with a wealthy man is because of his money.'

'This isn't about me,' Theo said icily. He raised himself into a sitting position so that they were now directly facing one another. 'And there's no point trying to swing the conversation in the opposite direction. There's just you and me here so let's cut to the chase. I will never allow you to marry Michael.'

Abby's mouth fell open in shock. No beating about the bush here.

'You may not have got around to talking about dates, but I suspect that's simply because you don't want to be seen to be rushing him into anything. Michael might well be gullible according to other people's standards, but I certainly don't consider him an idiot and nor, I imagine, do you. Alarm bells might just start ringing if you move from engagement to talk of marriage in too short a space of time.'

Abby had managed to close her mouth but her eyes were wide with disbelief as her brain sluggishly registered what he was saying. Gone was all pretence of politeness. Here was the fist of steel inside the velvet glove. There was not the slightest twinge of discomfort in the icy black eyes that were riveted to her face.

'You can't tell me who I can or can't marry,' was all she could find to say.

'I can when it affects my family. Beyond that I really don't care who you marry or what you do with your life.' He saw her soft mouth tremble and steeled himself against feeling like a pig because he had phrased his observation in the way that he had. She had had a weird, dysfunctional childhood but there was no way that she could still be sensitive to the passing remarks of strangers. It was all an act, he told himself, and the most appropriate way of dealing with it was to ignore it.

'I can't believe I'm hearing this,' Abby whispered.

'Of course you can,' Theo returned briskly. 'You must also have known that you'd come up against some resistance somewhere along the line. The thing I want to establish is how much it's worth to you to drop the engagement.'

He had originally thought that he could get to her, needle her somehow into dropping her cover, somehow force her hand so that Michael could see for himself the sort of woman that she was. Not to be.

'I don't understand what you're saying.' She shook her head in mute bewilderment even though she was already translating what he was saying insofar as it pertained to *her*.

Theo sighed. 'I've watched you with my brother. I have to admit I haven't noticed any passion there, but it's obvious that you two have some sort of friendly bond. I'm a fair man...'

'You? *Fair*?' A bubble of hysterical laughter began and died in her throat.

'Which is why,' Theo carried on as if she had not interrupted, 'I'm prepared to pay you handsomely for breaking off this engagement. I don't really care how you set about doing that but I'm sure you'll be able to think of something. You strike me as a very creative type of woman. It's a solution that works for all concerned. I go away safe in the knowledge that I'm sparing my brother a lifetime of disillusionment when you decide to divorce him at a later date. I'm giving you the option of maintaining a friendship with Michael until such time as you can gradually drift out of his life, and you get something for your co-operation. Face it, whichever way you look at it, I'm being staggeringly generous.'

The blood rushed to Abby's face in a wave of furious colour. She could feel every nerve in her body throbbing as she leaned forward and hit him on his face. Hard.

CHAPTER FOUR

MICHAEL had treated her to the dress she was wearing to the party. He had insisted. He wanted her to look beautiful and, after politely listening to her insist that she could get a perfectly good something or other at one of the department stores, had reasonably pointed out that something or other from a department store just wouldn't do. They would be surrounded by the Great and the Good, and she would just end up feeling awkward in something cheap and cheerful.

Abby now stood in front of the full-length mirror in the room and inspected her reflection joylessly.

The rich burgundy-coloured dress looked as stunning on her as it had when she had first tried it on at Harrods. Better, in fact, because she was wearing make-up, high heeled shoes and was clutching a little bag which was unnecessary but looked very elegant.

She twisted so that she could have a view of the back which, very daringly for her, plunged almost down to the waist, although the front was deceptively modest, with soft small folds camouflaging the fact that she was bra-less. It seemed odd to be wearing a long dress in a hot place, but the soft fabric against her legs felt very cool.

She would make everyone's head spin, Michael had assured her before he had gone to meet all the assorted friends and relatives who were arriving in batches. Abby could think of one notable exception but she had refrained from saying anything, just as she had avoided telling him about his brother's kind offer to buy her off.

She sighed now and continued standing where she was, reluctant to go outside but knowing that she couldn't remain hovering in the bedroom for much longer. It was already seven-thirty and the party had officially begun half an hour previously. She had telephoned England and spoken to Jamie, but not even the sound of his voice could still the tense, furious knot in the pit of her stomach.

Theo would only be on the island for one more day. Less, in fact. He would be leaving the following afternoon, and it would be easy to keep out of his way until then because the house was now full of guests overnighting. Most would leave the next day but, in the meanwhile, there would be sufficient people in which to lose herself.

The day's so-called sightseeing trip seemed to be on a circular tape in her head, replaying endlessly, always concluding with his insulting offer of money to get her out of his brother's life. Slapping him had achieved nothing, apart from granting her a temporary sense of satisfaction.

'You are excused once for doing that,' Theo had grated, catching the offending hand in a vice-like grip and pulling her towards him. 'Once and no more. And if I were you,' he had continued coldly, 'I would give my proposition a great deal of thought because, trust me, you'll either leave with money in your pocket or you'll leave with nothing. But you'll leave.'

They had completed the drive back to the villa in stony silence. For most of the trip Abby had sat pressed against the door, staring out of the window. There seemed little point in trying to convince him that he was wrong about her.

'Oh, well, I guess I'd better make my appearance,' she

said to her reflection. 'And I won't be cowering in the shadows either.'

She exited the room with her head held high. A bully was only as powerful as he was allowed to be. Theo Toyas was accustomed to everyone bending over backwards to accommodate him. If he clicked his fingers they jumped to his command. If he frowned they scurried to curry favour. And if he threatened, well, they cowered in fear and obeyed on bended knee.

Abby had no intention of doing any of those things.

She emerged to find the huge central area alive with guests. Some she had met earlier on when she had returned from her disastrous day out, but many more she didn't recognise at all. She expected quite a few would have arrived some time in the late afternoon, when she had already retired to the room to recover from her verbal battering. These guests would not be staying. They would have come by boat or by helicopter and would be returning the same way.

Through the open patio door she could see many more people were milling about outside.

For a few seconds she had to resist the urge to turn tail and run, but then she made her legs move and headed towards the first person she knew, all the while looking around to see if she could spot Michael anywhere. Also to see if she could find Theo, just so she could make sure to locate herself somewhere far from him.

Waiters and waitresses, most of them somehow related to the two retainers, threaded their way among the guests with platters of savouries and glasses of champagne or orange juice. The noise levels reflected the mood. Lots of laughter and the warm conversation of people who hadn't seen one another for a long time and were catching up.

Abby had expected to feel the outsider and had braced herself for a night of polite smiles and casual drifting around in the absence of knowing anyone in particular, but within minutes she discovered that this was certainly not to be the case.

She was embraced with enthusiasm and interest. The women complimented her on her choice of dress, the middle-aged men made inappropriate remarks and laughed at their sense of humour. Most spoke excellent English, but with an accent.

Michael was nowhere to be seen, and as she made her way from one group to another, stopping to chat with all, she kept her eyes open for him.

She was peering around, wondering why on earth he couldn't have made more of an effort to look out for her, when a voice murmured into her ear precisely what she was thinking.

'My brother seems to need a few lessons on looking after his woman.'

Abby froze, inhaled on a sharp breath and slowly turned around to look at Theo.

He looked utterly and devastatingly handsome. Black trousers were a concession to the formality of the party, but the crisp white shirt was rolled to the elbows in defiance of everyone else who, at least at this stage of the proceedings, had maintained the full dress code of jacket and tie. He was also wearing a bow-tie, undone so that he could release the top few buttons of his shirt.

Where had *he* come from? He must have been lurking, ready to pounce, because she hadn't spotted him at all since she arrived.

'I don't need looking after and, anyway, do you know where Michael is?'

'Maybe not *looking after*,' Theo amended, 'but I would

have thought that as your fiancé he would have been sticking to your side like glue. Especially given the outfit.'

'What about my outfit?' Abby swallowed the remainder of her first glass of champagne, but it failed to relax her. Her body felt like a piece of elastic stretched to its fullest.

'So much skin exposed at the back,' Theo drawled in a voice that sent shivers racing up and down her spine. 'Makes a man wonder what's at the front.' He tilted his glass to his lips and drank some of the champagne, but his eyes never left her face.

'I'm sorry, but I really must go and find Michael.'

'Why? You seem to be coping beautifully without him around. Odd.'

'I don't see anything odd about it at all,' Abby said irritably.

'You're recently engaged. Shouldn't you be in the throes of engaged bliss? Barely capable of taking your hands off one another, never mind tearing yourselves apart for a second?'

'I didn't know you were the romantic kind of man who thought like that,' Abby replied, sidestepping the question because what he said made perfect sense. Under normal circumstances, Michael would be by her side, showing her off to his family.

'I'm the kind of man who certainly wouldn't let his woman out of his sight.'

'Things are different in England. Possessiveness died out in the Middle Ages.'

'Which probably explains why English women can be so unfeminine. Too much independence can be a very bad thing.'

'Oh, right.' Abby forgot that she was trying to track

Michael down so that she could somehow make eye contact with him and be rescued from the dangerously disconcerting man towering over her. 'All those suffragettes who fought for women's rights would just love to hear you saying that. You'd be lynched from the nearest tree. For your information, independence is desirable. In fact, as far as I'm concerned, only an insecure man needs to have a woman around catering to his every need and putting him on a pedestal above everything and everyone.' Lord, had she learnt the hard way not to put any man on a pedestal? She could give lectures on the subject!

'Oh, don't get me wrong. I believe in women's rights. In fact, I have no tolerance for employers who exploit the sex of their employees by trying to pay women less than their male counterparts for doing the same job. Nor do I think that women should curtsey every time their man comes into view. However, you are here on your own, you know precious few people. I might have expected your fiancé to pick up the slack and be by your side.'

The logic of what he was saying left Abby lost for words for a few seconds.

'Michael…' she began. 'I know that Michael wanted to meet lots of people. If I had insisted that he stick to me, then he would have, but that would have been unfair on my part. I'm happy to just drift along on the sidelines, anyway, watching everyone having a good time…'

'Is that what you do in England? When you two go to parties together? Drift along on the sidelines while my brother does his own thing?'

'We don't often attend parties,' Abby said cautiously. 'At least not like this. And, don't forget, Michael has precious little time for socialising. The restaurant business is pretty tireless and now that he's involved with a club, well, his hours are bizarre most of the time.'

'And that doesn't bother you?'

'I think we ought to go and mingle.'

'I'm merely curious.'

'Are you?' Abby said sarcastically. 'Or is this another nail you're getting ready to stick in my coffin? We've been through your suspicions. I don't see the point of standing here talking about them more. Nothing's going to change!'

'Whatever I might think about your motives in getting engaged to my brother, I'm still curious as to how you could contemplate marrying a man who would rarely be around, and certainly never during social hours.' He signalled for a waitress to come and then helped himself to two glasses of champagne, handing one to her.

Theo wasn't lying. He was genuinely curious. He was also, he reluctantly admitted to himself, dazzled by her radiance. Her hair gleamed against her dress with a life of its own, long, straight and unbelievably blonde. Her lack of curves, which should have detracted from her appeal, instead added to it, giving her a gamine sexiness that was even more alluring than anything more obvious. It amazed him to think that his brother had left her on her own.

If it had been him…

'People *do* get involved with men who don't keep normal hours…'

'I'm not talking about *people* as a generic species. I'm talking about *you*.'

Abby gulped down her champagne, gasping as the bubbles hit her throat and went racing through her. The alcohol warmed her face. Gut instinct was telling her to get away from Theo. There was nothing he could say to her that wasn't, somehow, aimed to home in lethally on any chink in her armour. He wanted her out of his brother's life and away from the possibility that she could somehow get her hands on some of the Toyas millions. It made her sick just to think about it. But there was something about the man, something dark and compelling, that made her go against the grain and remain where she was.

The two glasses of champagne on an empty stomach wasn't helping matters.

'People need space from one another.' Abby shrugged. The champagne was now taking her down memory lane, and her eyes darkened. 'It gives you the chance to take a step back and be unemotional about the person you're involved with.'

Theo gently swirled his glass of champagne but his eyes were riveted to her face.

'And you think that's a good thing?'

'Of course it is. It means that you don't end up making a fool of yourself and trusting someone who isn't to be trusted.' She caught herself and managed a tight smile. 'I mean, generally speaking.'

'Who was he?'

'I don't know what you're talking about.' The sound of laughter and voices seemed very distant, just background noise. The man had sucked her into his orbit and she could feel her heart hammering uncontrollably in her chest.

'Of course you do,' Theo said softly, with just the right amount of surprise in his voice that she would even consider denying the truth.

In the semi-lit darkness he was all shadows and angles. His masculinity still surrounded him like a force field, but it didn't feel threatening. It felt...

Abby shivered.

'Well?' Theo prompted. 'Who was he? Naturally you're not talking about Michael. So who *are* you talking about?' He sipped some of the champagne, the finest champagne money could buy, needless to say, and lazily watched her. It was fairly dark out here in the garden, with only the lanterns providing illumination, but her hair still shone like a beacon. He clenched the stem of the glass because for one crazy passing moment he wanted to reach out and touch that hair, just to see whether it felt as good as it looked.

'Oh, just someone I used to know. He turned out to be not the person I thought he was.' Abby gave a light, short laugh.

The passing moment of wanting to reach out and touch her hair changed into a violent urge to kill whoever had caused that disillusionment. He brought himself up sharply at the wayward tangent his thoughts had taken and reined them firmly back into place.

But he still wanted to know…

He experienced a stab of sharp annoyance when Michael sauntered up to them and flung his arm around her shoulders, pulling her against him.

'Isn't she the belle of the ball?' he asked his brother. 'And, by the way, Mama wants you to meet your future bride. Alexis Papaeliou.' He grinned wickedly and raised his glass in a toast. 'You can run, big brother, but you can't hide.'

Theo tried to smile but he wished his brother would get the hell away so that he could finish his conversation. He was no longer looking at her, but he was aware of her with every fibre of his being. It was…madness.

'Alexis Papaeliou…yes, I think the name was mentioned earlier on…'

'Just your type, Theo. Lots of tumbling dark hair and curves and a dress that leaves very little to the imagination. I'm surprised Mama hasn't hurried to find you so that she can introduce you two.'

Well, of course that type of woman would be his sort, Abby thought nastily. The full-on type without too much to speak of in the brains department.

Then she flushed at just how uncharitable she was being to someone she had never met. Her only excuse was that the man was vicious towards her so was it so surprising that she would be critical back? Even if her criticisms were all in her head?

'I don't have a *type*,' Theo said irritably.

'Of course you do!' Michael was in his element. When he relaxed, he relaxed in style, probably making up for the fact that he was on call for so much of his time. 'Remember that girl you brought back home when you were seventeen?' He looked down at Abby and gave her a teasing squeeze, then he said to her, *sotto voce* but loud enough to be clearly heard by his brother, 'Her name was Raquel, a real dark-haired beauty. Theo brought her home for all to meet and was seriously surprised when everyone objected because she was in her thirties! She had told him she was nineteen! It was only when she let on that she had a child that the truth came out!'

'She looked younger than her age,' Theo commented, fidgeting.

'Then there was Nora. Beautiful Nora. Curvy brunette. Trouble was she had a brain the size of a pea!'

'But other assets that were far from pea-shaped.' Theo smirked.

'Perhaps you should scamper over to meet Alexis,' Abby said with a straight face. 'We wouldn't want to keep you from a love-match, would we, Michael?'

Theo hesitated. Under normal circumstances, he would have been all too happy to meet the girl, but when he stared frowningly down at the blonde angel innocently staring back at him he felt crazily reluctant to leave.

Dammit, didn't he remember that this so-called angel was engaged to his brother?

They were even sharing the same room, the same bed! He must be losing his mind...thinking about his brother's fiancée...wondering...

Alexis Papaeliou was everything the doctor ordered. She was vivacious without being free-spirited, stunning in a fiery kind of way, intelligent whilst still being deferential. And utterly, utterly straightforward. She worked for her father's company and had never nurtured any ambitions to do anything else. Highly commendable, Theo thought, searching with his eyes and finding Abby, who had once again been deserted by Michael but seemed to be doing just fine amongst a group of the younger men. God, not only did he have to watch out for his brother, but he also had to give him some sound advice on how to handle his woman.

As the assorted crowd were invited inside for supper he listened to his companion stretch her wings by telling him about her hobbies. She enjoyed horse-riding, it appeared, and was thinking of doing an art course so that she could paint when she retired from active work to marry and have babies.

At this point Theo decided that the conversation was getting a little too hazardous for his liking. He thanked heaven that his mother wasn't within earshot because she would be milking the situation for all it was worth.

He hadn't been lying when he had once told his mother that he would go down the expected route by the time he was forty. It was a good age to marry and assume the responsibilities of having a family. With a good Greek girl, pretty much like the charming one whose name-plate he found was next to his.

Abby, he couldn't help noticing, was next to Michael at the same table. Too far to hear what she was saying but within easy eye range. And she seemed to be having a wonderful time. How much had she drunk? he wondered grimly. She was certainly engaging in hectic conversation with old papa Silvio sitting next to her, whose face hadn't been known to crack a smile in over twenty years, since his wife died. He was laughing now, Theo noted.

He was vaguely aware of Alexis asking him questions about himself, trying to engage him in conversation, at which point he dragged his eyes away from the object of his scowling attention and did his utmost to charm his companion. It was something he found remarkably easy to do, even though precious little was ever revealed about himself and, in fact, any direct questions were cleverly side-stepped.

Abby didn't seem quite so circumspect in her conversation. In fact, she was leaning across Silvio now, engaging one of his aunts in animated chat. Theo wondered whether she would be able to eat at all in between being the life and soul of the party.

Professional caterers had been flown in to handle the food, which was a formal meal. Several tables had been interspersed in the open garden to accommodate the eighty or so guests, and the food, Theo had to admit, was very good. It was also served with an efficiency that came from paying the best to produce their best.

It was hard to tell whether the assembled crowd enjoyed the high quality food as much as they enjoyed the high quality wines. Certainly over the course of the evening the level of noise grew in direct proportion to the level of alcohol imbibed.

Theo drank enough to appear sociable and then he stopped. Amusing to watch everyone else lose their head, but he himself had no intention of following suit.

It did, however, make for an amazing atmosphere when, at shortly before midnight, his grandfather tapped his spoon on crystal and gave a short but funny speech about reaching the grand old age of eighty. He paid tribute to the wonderful wife he had lost and graciously thanked each and every one for making the tremendous effort to get to the island so that they could celebrate his birthday with him.

The round of applause was rousing. Various people had a go at making speeches themselves, to great cheering. When the noise had died down, Michael, who had always been his grandfather's favourite, did his best to give a sober performance and nearly succeeded but for the booming hiccup at the end. That, likewise, met with great cheering.

'After all this,' Theo began, standing up and lifting his glass in one last toast to a man who had touched all their lives in some way, 'my few words can only come as an anticlimax…'

Far from it. Abby had consumed far more than she ever could remember in her life, but she was still aware of how powerful Theo's brief speech was. There were a couple of funny moments mentioned in passing, but it was impassioned and moving and when she glanced across the table it was to see Lina dabbing her eyes with her serviette.

As many of the crowd capable of standing stood to raise their glasses, so did she. For one split-second their eyes tangled and she felt a funny feeling rip through her.

Where had that come from? she wondered dazedly. She had made a point of not looking at him at all for the whole of the evening, even if she had been conscious of his presence there on the same table as her. Now, those eyes seemed to pierce straight through her and send her carefully built-up self-control into immediate meltdown. She had a sudden, graphic memory of him on the beach, with the sun glinting on his bronzed, powerful body, and overlaying that were images of him swimming in the pool, cutting through the water like a smooth moving missile.

Abby blamed the champagne. There had been a lot of it before the food was finally served and even when the champagne had stopped it had been replaced by wine. Her glass had been permanently topped up.

With the toasts out of the way, people began drifting off, some moving to embrace the old man before retiring, others heading towards the garden. A music system had been cleverly rigged up and, whoever the DJ was, he was certainly digging back through the archives as the sweet voice of Nat King Cole wafted on the breeze.

Abby cornered Michael and whispered whether it might not be time for them to retire.

'The night is still a pup.' He grinned back, giving her a hug. 'Darling, you were just brilliant. You look wonderful and you've captivated everyone.'

'Your speech is sounding a little slurred,' Abby said irritably. Out of the corner of her eye, she was aware of Theo moving away from the table with the brunette on his arm. She turned her back on both of them.

'Did you like my speech?'

'It was wonderful.'

'Let's have a dance and then if you're tired you can head back. I'm going to stay until the break of dawn.'

That was reasonable enough. They joined the others in the other vast area of garden that had become an outdoor dance floor. Couples were entwined and dancing very slowly to the music. Some, Abby thought with amusement, were definitely propping each other up. One sudden move and they would topple over. Her eyes scanned the darkness and rested on Theo, also dancing with the brunette and holding her very close to him indeed.

Abby's heart gave another little flip which was almost as irritating as the fact that she hadn't been able to stop herself from seeking him out. Would they be retiring together? she wondered fuzzily. The thought of it made her feel hot and bothered.

She allowed herself to be pulled into Michael's arms, and she rested her head on his shoulder. He was a wonderful dancer. Even drunk, his feet seemed to be programmed to do exactly what they should do and Abby let herself go with the flow.

She closed her eyes and was only dimly aware of one slow number flowing into another one. Michael, in one ear, maintained a disjointed running commentary on the evening, dishing out little titbits of gossip that made Abby smile. That was so like him. He gossiped in the nicest possible way.

Halfway through a song, just when her thoughts were beginning to drift, Theo's voice brought her up sharply. She had been so far away mentally that in her confusion it took a few seconds to realise that he was cutting in so that he could dance with her.

Before she could protest, Michael was obligingly stepping aside and the safe comfort of his arms was replaced by a leaner, harder and infinitely more dangerous kind of embrace. Abby felt her body tense and she stiffly tried to impose a few inches of space between them but the slowness of the music was not helping her manoeuvres.

'Relax,' Theo murmured in her ear. 'Your body has to co-operate with the music, not fight it.'

'Shouldn't you be dancing with your love-match brunette?' Abby responded tartly and he gave a low chuckle that sent shivers down her spine. Through the haze of her blurry mind, one thought was emerging very clearly and it was that this man was sexy—really, truly and devastatingly *sexy*. She was appalled to find her body responding to his nearness now. Her breasts had become acutely sensitive and she could feel her nipples straining through the dress as, without the barrier of a bra, they pressed and rubbed against his shirt.

'I don't believe *I* was the one who called Alexis my love-match,' Theo drawled in a low voice. 'Although I admit she *does* fit the right mould…'

'*The right mould?*' Abby pulled back so that she could try and see whether he was being funny at her expense or not, but he responded by pulling her closer against him. It was quite likely he could feel her heartbeat because the damned thing was thudding against her ribcage like a hammer drill.

'Of course. We Greek men are very traditional. Women like Alexis are perfect. The right background, the right family connections…also, she has the right ambitions in life. She wants to have babies and please her husband…'

'What a role model for the modern woman,' Abby said. He hadn't included beauty in his list but perhaps that was taken as a given, one of those things that the ideal woman for him would have to possess.

'And are you any better?' he whispered smoothly.

Abby felt too languid to argue. The night was warm,

the music was softly seductive and champagne was flowing through her bloodstream, not too much but just enough to dampen her hostility. 'No,' she said. 'I'm not, gold-digger that I am. For a minute there I forgot that I was supposed to be a vile, unscrupulous woman with nothing more on her mind than destroying someone's life for the sake of his bank balance. Really the sort of person you wouldn't want to release in the presence of the young, the helpless or the impressionable.'

Theo felt a kick of pleasurable adrenaline rush through his body. 'How do you do that?' he murmured.

'Do what?'

'When I first saw you stepping out of that taxi...'

'You mean you were *spying* on me?'

'Appreciating the scenery, as it happened. It was greatly improved by your arrival. You looked like a kid...but I'm discovering that you've got the tongue of a rapier...my brother might have a flair for wielding a knife in the kitchen but I can't believe you would ever cut him to shreds with your own verbal dexterity...is that a side you haven't shown him yet...hmm? Because I don't think Michael has the stamina to take it...'

'That's unfair!' Abby protested. 'You make me sound like a shrew and I'm not! Anyway, I'm tired. I think I'll head back to my room now.'

'If you look behind you, you'll find that Michael doesn't look like someone who's ready to retire to bed.'

'I'm not expecting him to. He'll be staying up until the very end. Don't tell me...it's just not *the Greek way*...' She sighed. 'Look, Michael's letting his hair down and he deserves it. He works all the hours under the sun in England...I certainly don't begrudge him wanting to have a good time while he's over here...'

'What an understanding partner you are...and would

you be so understanding if the free rein you give him encourages him to wander off and find himself a new woman…?'

Abby couldn't help it. She giggled. That certainly did the trick when it came to Theo releasing her, which he did promptly, drawing her to one side away from the dancing couples, so that he could look down at her with a frown.

'Share the joke?'

'I'm sorry. I didn't mean to giggle. It's all the drink. I'm not used to so much wonderful champagne and wine. It's gone to my head and what with my exhaustion as well…' Her gorgeous dress, which had made her feel coolly confident at the start of the evening, was beginning to cling. During one of the toasts she had been jostled and champagne had spilled over it and being outside in the garden had done very little for keeping it pristine at the hem. She had felt curiously alert only moments before when she had been dancing with Theo, but now she really did feel bedraggled and a little sticky.

Theo continued to look at her. She confused him, was confusing him now, and he didn't like that. He didn't know how to deal with it.

'You don't think that Michael would run off with someone else? You are so confident of your charms?'

Abby could feel herself sobering up fast. 'No, not at all…I told you…I'm tired, I'm not reacting the way I normally would…'

'I will walk you to your room.'

'No!' She backed away slightly.

'It is only proper that you be escorted to your room…' Theo glanced briefly to where his brother appeared to be telling a joke that involved lots of hand gestures and hysterical laughter. Well, his audience were certainly appreciating it. 'And it would be cruel to interrupt Michael when he seems to be in the middle of a captivating anecdote.'

Abby turned around and couldn't stop herself from smiling. When she faced Theo again the smile was still tilting the corners of her mouth. 'Honestly, he's such a kid. I bet he's begun one of his jokes and can't remember the punchline. Happens every time he has too much to drink.'

The look on her face...and that confused feeling again, this time sharper. Theo drew his breath in sharply. Under the soft artificial light of the lanterns her face was all knowing and gently amused. Or was that his imagination? When he looked harder, the smile was no longer there and she was pulling back, ready to head off.

He couldn't let her go. Not yet. And he couldn't work out why. He was leaving the island the following day and he knew that he needed to talk to her for just a bit longer. The urge was so strong that it rocked him to his very core and just for a minute he experienced something he had never felt before...he experienced a complete absence of self-control. For a split-second something else was controlling him and he didn't know why or how.

'I'll walk you to your room,' he repeated tightly and watched the pale delicacy of her neck as she turned away from him before shrugging as though resigned to something being thrust upon her. He shoved his fists into his pockets, knowing that somewhere out there in the shadows Alexis was probably watching and wondering why he was clearing off without a word to her. Thank goodness his mother and his grandfather had already retired for the night. He would have been hard-pressed to have explained why he was showing his brother's fiancée to her room and, worse, why he felt compelled to do so...

CHAPTER FIVE

'You look tired.' He noticed that she was making sure to keep distance between them, as much as was possible without scraping the wall next to her.

'I am. It's been a long day.'

Theo let a few seconds of silence stretch past. 'I suppose you're referring to our little sightseeing trip earlier on?'

Abby couldn't be bothered to respond to the jibe. While she had been at the party she had felt buoyant and keyed up and the alcohol had given her a flushed, excited feeling that had kept her going through the difficult task of mixing and mingling with Michael's relatives, people she had never met in her life before. Now that the evening was over, she felt drained. It didn't help that this man was walking next to her, escorting her to her bedroom like a security guard making sure that the guest didn't make off with the family heirlooms.

'I hope you understand why I have obvious concerns about you, Abby.'

'I really don't want to talk about this. Again. I'm tired and I just want to get to bed and go to sleep.'

Theo felt his hackles rise at the casual dismissiveness in her voice. His time on the island was virtually up and he had achieved nothing when it came to protecting his brother's millions. True, the woman had not been what he had expected, but he had not found a single foothold which he could have used as a cautionary tale to his mother and Michael. Nor had she risen to the tempting bait of being paid off.

And here she was, dismissing him.

'Won't Michael be disappointed to find his woman sleeping when he gets in from the mad festivities?'

'I don't think so.' Abby spied her door with some relief. The intricately sprawling villa, which had been virtually empty when she had arrived, was now full to bursting, a very comforting thought just at this point in time when Theo's unwanted presence was pressing down on her like an enforced intimacy, stretching every nerve in her body to tense breaking-point.

'I never asked,' Theo said casually. 'Do you and my brother live together?' That would account for the way they carelessly seemed to take one another for granted. It would also account for the ease with which she had rejected his financial carrot to disengage herself from Michael. No incentive there if she was already feasting off the spoils by way of a joint income in a joint house somewhere and, however much Michael was unmoved by money, his house would be nice. He liked beautiful things. He could have kicked himself for never having taken the time out to go and see for himself how his brother lived. It had always been convenient to have Michael travel to London to see *him*. That way, he had never had the need to interrupt his working life too much. As it was, he could only imagine the luxury in which Abby was basking.

'No, we don't, as a matter of fact. Okay, well, thank you so much for walking me to my room, although I suspect I would have got here safe and sound by myself.' She stood with her back to the door and delivered a bright smile.

'You don't live together? I confess I'm surprised.'

With a movement so accomplished that Abby was un-aware of it being done, Theo reached behind and pushed open the bedroom door, then insinuated himself inside the room before she had time to open her mouth in pro-test.

Now it was his turn to face her. 'I didn't think that the conventions of separate living quarters still applied in this day and age when two people are engaged.'

Behind him, the single lamp on the chest of drawers illuminated the sofa which Michael had used earlier on to have a quick nap on, and which neither of them had bothered to remake.

They had both been scrupulous in keeping up appear-ances since they had arrived. Before the room was cleaned, all evidence of sofa occupation had been eradi-cated. Just in case. Housekeepers had a habit of gossiping and gossip had a habit of spreading.

Why they hadn't had two separate rooms, Abby had no idea, but Michael's reasoning had been that his grand-father would have been startled at that arrangement. More so than his mother, and certainly Theo would have been more than startled. Back in England, it had seemed pretty easy to fit in with his plans.

With one disarranged sofa staring her in the face, com-plete with rumpled pillows, Abby felt her stomach go into cramp mode.

She stayed put in the doorway and linked her hands behind her back. Nervous, fidgeting hands told a story of their own. 'I'm accustomed to living in my own space,' Abby blurted out, tearing her eyes away from the wretched sofa. 'I have all my things around me…and besides, with Michael's working hours, it's not as if we would be spending all our evenings together watching television and pottering in the kitchen…' She thought of

Jamie, running around her townhouse, scattering toys in the sitting room. One more thing to be kept under wraps. Thank God the man was leaving later on that day.

'But it would have been more convenient, surely, not to have the expense of keeping on two places…?'

'I guess. Well…' She yawned and took a small step backwards to psychologically encourage him to follow suit. He stayed put.

'Where are you going?'

'I beg your pardon?'

'You're going backwards, Abby.' He reached forward and switched on the overhead light and, in the same motion, swung round and stepped aside.

Abby reluctantly stepped into the room and followed the direction of his curious gaze. The sofa could not have shown more indication of its occupancy. Two pillows, still bearing the imprint of Michael's head, cushions tossed on the carpet, and, as the final touch, a sheet carelessly screwed up down one end. The bed, on the other hand, was untouched.

'Well, well, well…' Theo strolled forward, picked up the cushions and placed them randomly on the sofa, then he turned to her and folded his arms. 'Little domestic tiff, perhaps?'

'Have I told you how tired I am?'

'Several times.'

'If you had an ounce of decency you'd take the hint and go. But then we both know that you and decency are not words that go together in the same breath.'

'Curiouser and curiouser…' The wolfish smile sent a shiver of apprehension racing up and down Abby's spine. She drew herself up and gave him her coldest stare, but her mind was a blank. 'So explain…'

'There's nothing *to* explain. Michael wanted a nap and the sofa seemed as good a place as any.'

'Even with a king-sized bed only feet away? Are you telling me that my brother is a masochist?'

'I don't have to tell you anything at all!'

Theo advanced towards her, backing her against the wall. He then proceeded to lean against the wall, resting on one arm and efficiently blocking her exit with the other. 'You're not sleeping with my brother, are you?'

'That's a ridiculous assumption!' *Ridiculous?* It was a natural conclusion. If the shoe was on the other foot she would have thought exactly the same thing. She could have kicked herself for not tidying up the room before she left, but she had been so flustered, her mind wandering on to other things, that she had barely noticed the telling disarray. Nor, it had to be admitted, had she expected anyone else to go inside the room, least of all the man towering over her now.

'I must say I'm asking myself *why*…'

'Get out!' Abby demanded desperately. 'Or else I'll…'

'Scream? Slap me again? Stamp your feet…?'

'Does my brother not attract you…?' He didn't know why, but that gave him a tremendous surge of well-being. He could see the wariness underneath the glare and he felt the satisfaction of knowing that he had cornered her. Not in the way he had originally imagined, but he had definitely cornered her.

And she wasn't sleeping with Michael.

'Well?' he prompted.

'I'm not going to answer any of your questions and if Michael knows that you've been bullying me…'

'Me? Bullying you? I'm showing a healthy interest. Why are you and my brother sharing a room if you're not even sleeping together? Maybe…' His eyes gleamed darkly. 'Maybe you prefer tantalising him with your body…look but don't touch…'

'That's disgusting!'

'You think so?' Theo seemed distracted for a few seconds. Abby could work out without too much difficulty what sort of images were occupying his mind, images of women performing stripteases for his own private pleasure, she thought waspishly.

'Or maybe,' he mused, enjoying this little game of discovery, 'the fact that you're not attracted to my brother makes no difference to you at all.'

Abby was aware of her heart beating and the fine film of perspiration that was making her skin tingle. She had never felt so trapped in her life before and, while common sense was telling her that whatever Theo Toyas said it would all be speculation, she still felt the fear of the hunted slowly being circled by the predator.

Theo was not at all deterred by her silence. He no longer knew whether he was driven by a need to protect his brother, which had certainly been his aim at the start, or by an even more powerful and baffling need to find out about the slight woman standing there, locked effectively in his cage. Her eyes were wide and cautious but the superficial calm of her features was betrayed by the pulse beating rapidly in her neck. He would have liked to have touched that pulse, feathered his finger over it…

'I don't care what you think, Theo…'

'Of course you do.'

'Why? Why should I? Just because everyone you ever meet is interested in what you have to say, doesn't mean that *I* am.'

'You might not *want* to be interested, but you are, because I am Michael's brother, because whether you like it or not Michael does not live in a vacuum. You claim that you have no interest in my brother's money. If that was the case, then why are you conducting a relationship with him when you're not attracted to him?'

'I never said I wasn't attracted to Michael. I think he's exceedingly attractive, as a matter of fact.'

'But not attractive enough to get you into bed. I believe in consideration between two consenting adults, but isn't that taking it a bit too far? And what happens when my brother decides that the time has come to stop playing the gentleman? Do you then insist on the wedding ring on the finger? Is that where your feminine modesty springs from? A more pedestrian need to keep Michael on his toes, dangling the carrot in front of him so that you have him where you really want him? Very clever. The chase is always so much more enticing than the actual catch...'

Abby raised her hand, anger and panic guiding her, but this time there was no connection with that arrogant face. Instead he deftly caught her wrist and held it.

'Uh huh. You've done that once and it's once too often as far as I'm concerned.' He pulled her slightly towards him and felt the atmosphere change with electric speed.

Her breathing quickened and her pupils dilated. It no longer seemed to matter whether he had been attacking her or not. Her mind might have been responding to what he had been saying, but her body was responding to *him*. That one certainty rushed through him on a wave of powerful force. Theo felt his mouth go suddenly dry as he was caught up in a vortex of similar *wanting*, because there was no other word to describe what he was feeling. Suspicion and curiosity melded together into shattering animal attraction.

A succession of images whizzed through his head, starting from his first look at her, unobserved, as she had emerged from that taxi, and ending with how she looked tonight.

'You make me want to slap you!' Abby said in a strangled voice. His dark eyes were piercing her, burning a hole in her defences and his mouth…she looked at his mouth and hurriedly looked away.

'What else do I make you want to do, Abby?' he murmured softly. In the intensity of the moment, Michael was just an image, rapidly receding.

'I don't know what you mean,' Abby stammered. 'You've got me all wrong.'

'You know what I mean.' He released her wrist but he didn't step back. Instead, he enfolded her in an embrace in which no physical contact was made because he wasn't touching her at all, just leaning against the wall over her, supporting himself on the flat of his hands, elbows bent so that he was only inches away.

Abby felt as though she was slowly suffocating. But she liked the feeling. It was so intense and so blindingly *real*. With a jolt, she realised how successfully she had managed to withdraw from all meaningful contact with the opposite sex over the years. She chatted, she went out in a group, but no one ever got very close. The doors she had always had open to the world had been firmly sealed and locked. It was just mystifying how this one man, the least suitable man in the world for a host of reasons, had managed to prise them open.

Her lips parted on a desperate protest but nothing emerged. She was aware of him leaning down and then the only sound she heard herself make was a groan as his mouth covered hers and his hands reached to cup her face, tilting it so that her whole body was arched up to receive his kiss.

A couple of minutes, if that, when she was lost. All

the needs and urges that had dried up inside her flared into sudden, breathless life. She responded with every ounce of her being as his tongue invaded her mouth like something seeking to reach straight into her soul.

Then lessons learnt and years of self-preservation rushed back into focus. And with it the image of Michael.

She pushed hard, struggling to free herself, gasping like someone deprived of oxygen.

Theo withdrew immediately. Her fabulous blonde hair was tangled around her face and he resisted smoothing it back, angry with himself because he hadn't wanted it to end. He had wanted to take them both to their destination.

Now Michael's face rose up accusingly and his anger shifted on to her.

'How dare you?' Abby demanded.

'Bit late in the day for self-righteous anger, don't you think?' he ground back at her. 'Michael doesn't do it for you, does he? Or maybe you've just decided that I'm the better catch? Hmm?'

'That's a despicable thing to say!'

'But then I'm despicable, as you keep saying. Yet not so despicable that you don't melt when I touch you.' He pushed himself away, knowing that he now had the ammunition to do what he had wanted to do from the start, to provide ample proof to his brother that his beloved fiancée was not the pure young thing he obviously mistook her for.

He could, he knew, wrap it all up before he left to return to Athens. She would then be out of his brother's life for ever and he would never have to clap eyes on her again.

'I…'

'You…? Carry on. I'm all ears…'

'You should leave now.'

'Is that all you have to say?'

'Michael will be here any minute…'

'Don't pretend that you give a damn about my brother or about what he thinks! You've just proved to me exactly how much you care about him!'

For a few tense seconds neither said a word. The air was thick with regret and accusations and with the lingering remnants of lust which Theo was finding frustratingly difficult to get out of his system. She looked away and his eyes were drawn to the fragile pallor of her skin and the vulnerable way she was clasping her hands together, as if trying to steel herself from shaking all over like a leaf.

He was assailed with the treacherous thought that if he had had to find out about her this way, then he would have wanted to go the whole distance, to scoop those breasts out and taste them, to yank down the dress and expose every inch of her nudity. He stifled the guilty, distasteful thought but his painful erection still told him what he didn't want to hear.

'I'll do you the favour of not being the one who provides this piece of proof to Michael about your duplicity. I'll leave it to you to break off the engagement of your own free will, in whatever manner you see fit.'

'Big of you, but how do you know that I want to do that? Or that Michael would, even if you went to him and told him about…well…one kiss…'

This wasn't what Theo had expected to hear. 'My brother might be fooled by pretty words and simpering looks, but I don't think my mother or my grandfather would take a similar view and, in case you haven't noticed, my brother holds them both in very high regard.'

Abby flushed. 'Okay.'

'And don't even think of trying to pull a fast one.'

'Such as what?'

'Such as keeping quiet or, worse, bringing forward plans for the white wedding. It won't work. I'm in Athens for the next few weeks, but as soon as I'm done there I'll damn well get in touch with Michael and make sure that you've done precisely what I've told you to.' He walked towards the door and pulled it open, then he turned to her. 'I bet you're wishing now that you had accepted my original offer to disappear with your pockets lined…'

Abby whitened but kept silent. What was the use of any retort? She only realised how rigidly tense she was once he had gone, softly closing the door behind him just like a clandestine lover would have.

Then her whole body sagged. She could barely bring herself to go to the bathroom, to go through all the motions of getting undressed, getting into her night clothes, removing her make-up. But she did, operating on automatic pilot like a robot. Having cursed Michael earlier on, when it had become clear that in his absence Theo was going to walk her to her room, she now prayed that he wouldn't return in a hurry. Her thoughts were so chaotic that she felt that he might take one look at her and read every one of them.

And the most sinful of all those thoughts were the ones of what she had felt when Theo Toyas had touched her. All the awareness she had stored up unconsciously had rushed out at her, like a flood bursting through the fragile walls of a badly made dam. She had wanted him so badly that her body had felt as though it were on fire, a great raging fire that started deep inside her and radiated outwards, devouring every scrap of common sense in its rampaging path.

Under the comfort of the light blanket she shivered convulsively in the darkened room and whimpered.

If she kept her eyes open she heard his voice, his dark, seductive voice leading her astray so that he could turn on her with his vicious accusations. If she closed her eyes she could see him and see her reaction to him, like a third party spectator witnessing a huge error of judgement taking place in slow motion.

Why had she not fought him off? No, she wouldn't even have had to fight him off, she knew that. He was not a man to pursue his interests in the face of opposition, not when it came to a woman. One hint of reticence on her part and he would have sensed it, would not have made a move. She could hardly blame the alcohol level in her blood. Her head had never felt clearer.

She hadn't fought him off because she had been desperate to touch him and to have him touch her.

The acceptance of that fact made her moan softly into the covers. She felt stripped bare. All the defences she had painstakingly built up over the years had been knocked down in one fell swoop and in the most dramatically awful way possible.

Of course she would tell Michael but there was an ache inside her at the thought that Theo would get what he wanted, what he had set out to get from the very start, and he would vanish out of her life believing her to be the woman he had conjured up in his head. A cold-blooded gold-digger who had trapped his brother and who would have gone to the final limit had he not managed to trick her into virtual self-confession. He would congratulate himself on a job well done. Where words hadn't worked, action had spoken.

Sleep eventually overtook her but it was a restless sleep. She imagined that she would tell Michael what had happened the following day but, with utter predictability, he was so deeply asleep when she finally woke up at a little after nine in the morning that Abby didn't have the heart to wake him. And what good would her confessions do at this point in the holiday, anyway? He would spend the rest of his short break on tenterhooks. Better, she decided, to leave it until they returned to England.

The villa, as she had expected, was full of activity. People were leaving and the huge open tiled hall was full of various holdalls. Lina was busily clucking around everyone, making sure that the transport they had arranged had arrived on time. Abby melted into the jumble of mostly hung-over guests, smiled and made sensible remarks about how successful the party was, kissed cheeks and uttered the right noises about hoping to meet again. She would have liked to, she thought. All these friends and relatives were a lively, interesting bunch and it had been wonderful being part of one great big family for a short while. Having had nomadic parents who had never even put down roots when she had been a child, it was a wonderful eye-opener to be confronted by this huge group who had. Uncles and aunts and cousins and nieces and nephews all knew one another and many knew the friends of friends of each other.

Fortunately the one key member of the group whom she didn't want to see was not around. Theo had probably slept in as well or maybe he was working, getting back into the mindset to return to business now that the obligatory party was out of the way and his mission to free his brother from the claws of the gold-digger had been accomplished.

Without any transport to remove her from the villa, Abby made do with grabbing some breakfast and then retreating to the furthest part of the garden with her book and her thoughts.

The garden was vast enough to easily locate a hiding place. There were trees, plants and shrubs and benches scattered around, inviting people to sit and take a rest. Abby located one furthest from the house and went through the motions of opening her book, but her brain refused to assimilate the words on the page in front of her.

It had been years since she had touched a man, kissed him, had felt that drive surge through her, making her want to hold him naked against her.

That it had happened at all was frightening. That it had happened with Theo Toyas was terrifying.

The black print on the page in front of her blurred over and Abby blinked, clearing her eyes and telling herself that she wouldn't cry. Instead, she gave up on the pretext of trying to read and lay back on the wooden lounging chair and closed her eyes. The breeze was soft and warm. Somewhere back at the villa guests were departing, but it was impossible to hear any voices from where she was, hiding in the depths of the carefully cultivated garden. If Michael's grandfather had fashioned the villa to celebrate his young wife, then he had obviously done so with a youthful enthusiasm for privacy under the open sky.

Having had precious little sleep the night before, Abby could feel her eyelids getting heavier and she welcomed the peace of not having to think, not having to beat herself up with recriminations over her own stupidity.

She had no idea how long she had been sleeping and no idea how much longer she would have slept for had she not been awakened by the sound of something out of place, the sound of something that wasn't the breeze rustling through the leaves. Her eyes fluttered open to find that she was in shade and not because the sun had dipped behind a cloud.

Theo was looming over her and she struggled to find some composure.

Her heart began to thud and creeping colour stole into her cheeks. He was vitally masculine in a pair of light cream trousers and a thin cotton shirt in faded blues and greys. His hair was damp and swept back from his face. Even with every sense leaping into immediate defence she was still aware of the primitive tug he exercised over her body. It was an instinctive reaction over which she seemed to have no control and it was even more terrifying now because somehow the light of day made it starkly real.

'What do you want?' she asked tersely, pushing herself up into a sitting position. 'How did you find me here?'

'I thought of the most obvious place you would go to hide away from the possibility of bumping into me.'

Abby didn't bother to beat about the bush. 'Can you blame me?'

Theo appreciated the blunt honesty. He gave her a slow smile that did weird, wonderful, scary things to her stomach even though her expression remained coldly hostile. 'No, I can't say that I do,' he drawled.

'So why have you come to find me? You've done what you wanted to do, haven't you?'

'Have I? Have you told Michael yet? That your love match is off?'

'No, I haven't.'

'Why?'

'Because he's still sleeping! It would be hard to have a conversation with someone who isn't awake!'

This time Theo's smile was genuine. He had to hand

it to her. The girl was gutsy and funny underneath that butter-wouldn't-melt-in-your-mouth exterior.

'Poor Michael. Sleeping the sleep of the innocent. Not to mention the frustrated. When do you intend to break the news?'

'When we get back to England.' She was shielding her eyes from the glare so that she could look up at him. It gave her a small advantage insofar as he couldn't read her expression and, as though clocking on to that fact, he squatted down so that now he was on eye level with her, his face only inches away from hers.

'Good,' he said, silkily amenable, 'because I wouldn't want you to forget that I'll be checking up to make sure that you have.'

'Are you leaving now?' Abby asked politely. 'Because I wouldn't want to keep you.'

'Wouldn't you?' Theo murmured. 'Yes, I am off now. Business is a beast that never sleeps.'

'Leaving on your own?' She had meant to leave him with the parting jibe that if he was leaving in the company of Alexis, then maybe he should spend a little time examining his own morality, but before she could launch into her invective he threw her another of those lazy smiles that made her toes curl and the hairs on the back of her neck stand on end.

'Yes, I am. Why? Did you think that I might be leaving with the delectable Alexis?' He shook his head with regret. 'She wants too many things I'm not willing to provide at this point in time. Declarations of love, rings with large diamonds and the distant sound of wedding bells chiming over the horizon.'

'You mean you just prefer to sleep around,' Abby said scornfully.

'You call it sleeping around,' Theo said with a glint

in his eye. 'I call it dealing honestly with members of the opposite sex. I don't make promises I have no intention of keeping.' At this rate, he would miss the meeting he had scheduled for later in the afternoon. The private island hopper waiting for him would continue to wait, but his meeting involved several highly influential and very busy financiers for whom time was money and wasted time was close to a cardinal sin. 'Why are you interested?' he asked. 'Are you jealous?'

'Jealous?' Abby spluttered, outraged. 'You really are the most arrogant, egotistic human being I have ever met!'

'You haven't answered the question, though...' Her softly parted mouth was an invitation he couldn't resist and this time there was no guilt attached. She wasn't sleeping with Michael. She was using him. That she hadn't come right out and admitted it was simply a small matter of technicality.

He breached the short space between them and covered her mouth with his, felt it again, that confusion of anger and wanting that had been there in her before, when he had kissed her the previous night. The knowledge that she wanted him even though she hated herself for it was like adrenaline flooding his system. He felt his hard, aching erection bulging against his zipper and he continued to ravish her mouth with his. Acquiescence came when she wound her arms around his neck and when he reached to slide his hand under the small cropped top there was just a groan of submission. She wasn't wearing a bra. She obviously had no idea that although her breasts were small they were perfectly formed and liable to drive any red-blooded male to distraction. How his brother could occupy the same space as her and keep his hands to himself was beyond him. He had to see. Hang the meeting. So he might be slightly late. They would be peeved but they would wait because he was too powerful for them to walk away.

He pushed up the top and was hotly turned on. Her nipples were large pink circles standing proudly, the tips stiffly erect, calling him to take one into his mouth just to suck, just to taste, and to hear her fevered response.

Abby squirmed as he suckled her nipple, caressing the other breast with his hand, making sure that there were no nerve-endings in her body that weren't sizzling. He teased, pulling the aroused bud into his mouth, sending all her thoughts into free fall. Never, never had she felt like this before.

Her fingers tangled in his hair and she pushed him down, not wanting him to stop his fevered explorations.

It was only when his hand moved down to claim that one place which was now damp with desire that reality crashed through the barriers of her fevered mind and she wriggled frantically against him, trying to yank down her top with one hand and push him away with the other.

'No!' She dragged herself upright and looked at him with shocked eyes. Her top was now back in place but her nipples were still throbbing from where he had assaulted them with his mouth and her whole body was trembling.

It took a few seconds for Theo to register the cooling distance between them and only a few more for him to realise just how out of control he had been. What the hell had just gone on? he wondered dazedly. He pushed himself up, aware of his erection, which was still clamouring for satisfaction. There she was, all pink-faced and appalled. Had he gone mad?

'A little reminder,' he said, grateful that his voice at

least betrayed nothing of what he was feeling, 'of why you need to break off your engagement.'

With that parting shot he turned on his heel and walked away and Abby watched his departing back and wondered how, having suffered all manner of mortification the night before, she had allowed herself to do the same again. The warning bells were ringing so loudly in her head that she felt faint. When she finally got to her feet, safe in the knowledge that he would have left for sure, it was to find that they were still shaking.

He was gone, she told herself over and over, gone for good and thank God for that.

CHAPTER SIX

'HAVE you heard from your brother?'

Abby looked at Michael, who was lying prostrate on her sofa. Sundays were the only days he enjoyed away from work and, aside from the occasional lunchtimes when they would meet for something to eat during the week, they both tried to do something on Sundays. Today had been a day in the Pavilion Gardens, which Jamie had enjoyed. The weather had been beautiful and they had taken a picnic lunch, which Michael had done and, with his usual flair, had produced superb food for the three of them and the other six who had come along as well. Of course, it hadn't been quite as carefree for Abby because Jamie demanded so much of her attention, but everyone had chipped in and, without a child between them in sight, had enjoyed the novelty of someone else's.

And Jamie had enjoyed being the centre of attention. It was difficult for him and she knew that. He was getting to the age where he had begun asking questions about why he had no father, and she knew that those questions would probably become more pressing over time.

She had become lost in her thoughts when she was abruptly pulled back into the present by Michael saying that he had.

'You have?' Instantly she was on the alert. It had been three weeks, and she had already begun to think that maybe Theo would have forgotten his threat to be in touch, to make sure that the engagement had been broken off to his satisfaction. She had lulled herself into thinking that things that had seemed so real and so important in Santorini might have faded into the background under the frantic grind of his daily life. It wasn't as though he had lots of free time on his hands to mull over his brother's situation. 'What did you tell him? He's not coming down here, is he?' She knew that her voice was laced with panic. Just as she had managed to bury her head in the sand about Theo's threats, so too had she diminished his huge impact on her, telling herself that she had imagined her heated, mindless responses, that it had all been the effect of her nerves and the disorientation of being in another country, away from her son and her normal pace of life.

Now that hard, arrogant, ridiculously sexy face rose up from the mists of her memory like a punch in the gut.

'He can't come here, Michael. I don't want to see him.'

'You mean you're scared to see him.' Michael propped himself up on one elbow and grinned. 'Oh, the tangled webs we weave!'

'It's not funny!'

'It is when you sit back and look at it. There we were, blithely making our plans, and you end up falling for my brother. Who could have predicted that? No—' he gave the matter a few seconds' thought '—I could have predicted that. He's had that effect on women roughly from the day he was born. He was a charmer then and he's a charmer now. I warn you, though…you're better off not getting entangled with him. He's the proverbial heartbreaker.'

'Tell me something I haven't already figured out for myself,' Abby scoffed. She stood up, utterly at ease in her dreadful slumming-it-at-home outfit of loose checked pyjama bottoms that never seemed to fit on her waist but a few inches below, and the sleeveless red vest that had seen more vibrant days.

It was a little after eight in the evening. Jamie was sound asleep upstairs, thoroughly worn out after a day of running about madly, and she had no plans to leave the house. Chances were that Michael might well end up staying on the sofa-bed. There was a movie on at nine-thirty which they both wanted to watch and often enough he simply stayed the night if he considered it too much effort to leave for his own penthouse apartment over-looking the coastline.

'And I haven't *fallen for him*. He's arrogant and ob-jectionable.'

'But hugely irresistible to the opposite sex.'

'I made a mistake. How many times have *you* done that?'

'Too many to mention, my sweet, but then I'm not you.'

Abby decided to sidestep this line of conversation. Michael knew her just a little too well for her own good. 'What did you tell him?'

'Not a great deal, as it happens. He called last night when I was in the middle of trying to sort out some hideous fiasco with the shrimps and I couldn't stop for a long chat.'

'Did he ask whether we were still engaged?'

'I presume he's waiting for me to volunteer the infor-mation.'

Abby took a few seconds to digest this. As far as Theo was concerned, she was going to be responsible for let-ting Michael down gently, presumably with no mention of what had happened between them. It would therefore have seemed strange had he come right out and asked whether they were still together when he would have had no reason to ask the question in the first place.

'And what are you going to tell him?'

'No idea.' He lay back down on the sofa and stared up at the ceiling.

Abby looked feverishly at his unruffled face.

'I don't like lying,' he said eventually, 'but I know Mum will be worried sick if she thinks that I'm no longer an engaged man. She'll have images of me dying of a broken heart in my apartment with nothing for company but empty vodka bottles and the television. And my grandfather isn't very well at the moment. We're all hoping that it's just a case of the party being a little too much for him, but...' His expression was worried when he looked at her and Abby felt a swift tug of compassion. 'Theo's concerned about him and Theo is never concerned unless there's a valid reason. I told him that I would meet him in London some time next week. Maybe I can just skirt around the engagement thing, deal with it later...'

Skirt around...? Deal with it later...? Those were words she didn't associate with Theo Toyas, but she uneasily plucked the one comforting piece of information from Michael's conversation. He would be going to London to see his brother. There would be no need for her to go with him and she had no intention of doing so.

'So you haven't actually set a date to meet...?'

Michael shook his head. 'When Theo comes over here on business it's next to impossible pinning him down to any specifics when it's got nothing to do with work. Unless, of course, you happen to be his woman of the moment, in which case I expect he makes time...though I wouldn't lay money on it...' There was a certain reluctant admiration in Michael's voice at the sheer ruthless-

ness of his brother's habits. Abby refused to accommodate the emotion.

'Charming man, your brother.'

'Charming enough to…'

'Don't even think of saying it, Michael.' She picked
up the cushion which was lying on the ground by her
chair and flung it at him.

It was funny, but even Michael, for all his intuition,
didn't know how deeply Theo had affected her. He knew
her well enough to know that she would not have kissed
him on a sudden whim, but he also thought that she was
controlled enough to have put it behind her. She would
never have dreamt of confessing to him how much it still
played on her mind. She would catch herself thinking
about Theo, remembering the way he had kissed her, and
in between laughing it off to herself would still feel dis-
turbingly aware that she wasn't putting it behind her the
way she should have been able to.

'Let me know when you go and how it goes,' she said,
blinking away the unwelcome thoughts. Talking about
Theo like this, knowing that Michael would be seeing
him some time in the next week, made her shiver.
Knowing that he would be in the same country, looking
up at the same sky, made her shiver.

'Which is what I've got to do.'

'What?'

'Go.' He heaved himself off the sofa with a deep sigh
and in between her protests explained that he would be
going to the club to make sure that everything was going
all right. There was a new act performing, he told her,
talking and putting on his shoes at the same time. A jazz
band from Edinburgh, some new guys. He wanted to
keep an eye on them, see whether they were good enough
to hire again. He needed to keep the punters happy and

Brighton had so many clubs that his had to excel to compete. Abby protested, but half-heartedly. It had been an exhausting day and she would be glad to get into bed.

She had seen him to the door and was switching off the lights in the kitchen when the doorbell rang. Abby flew out to the small hallway. The doorbell was particularly penetrating and it had a nasty habit of waking Jamie up. Once awake, Jamie could remain awake for hours, with his body telling him it was time to play even if his brain was informing him that it was time to sleep.

She pulled open the door and there he was.

So tall, so sexy and so unexpected that for a few seconds all she could do was blink, as if blinking would make the man there disappear or else turn him into Michael.

Her brain finally caught up with her vocal cords. 'What are you doing here?'

'I was just passing by,' Theo drawled. 'Thought I'd look in.' He looked lazily past her and then right back at her, his face a study in self-contained impassivity.

Abby, on the other hand, was struggling to breathe.

'You can't be here,' she whispered incredulously. 'You don't know where I live.'

'I knew where you lived the minute I found out where you worked. You don't have to be Sherlock Holmes to make a call to an office and dig out relevant information.'

'Personnel would never have given you my address!'

'And why not? You forget that I'm Michael's brother. I don't suppose you want to invite me in but you are going to have to, you know, because I don't intend to stand out here having a conversation, however nice the weather.'

'You're seeing Michael next week. He told me. Why do you want to see me now? Why?'

'Oh, but you know why. If you don't move I'm going to have to pick you up and move you.'

Abby looked at him with dismay. He had managed to stick his foot just inside the threshold. If she tried to slam the door on him it would entail a struggle and she would lose. She was no match for Theo Toyas. She stood aside and watched him walk into her house and look around him with curiosity and interest.

The house was the smallest of two-bedroomed properties. She had bought it six years previously, taking out the largest possible mortgage she was allowed and, by being sensible, she had managed to sustain it. It was on a small development close to a primary school and there were just about enough amenities to make it a first time buyer's first port of call on the property ladder. The houses were like boxes, but pleasant enough boxes and, depending on size, all had a pretence of a garden. In her case, it was a small patch of grass outside her back patio door which she cultivated with creative zeal.

She would have liked to have been bold with her décor inside the house, maybe have some unusual colour schemes to lift it out of its bland mediocrity, but her original forays into reds and deep greens had been a disaster. The house was too small to take kindly to unusual colour schemes and, in the end, she had regretfully settled on whites, creams and a very adventurous toffee in the hallway. Only the bedrooms reflected any real vibrancy. Jamie's was a high, attractive turquoise and she had taken time to paint the flat-packed bedroom furniture in a wonderful shade of yellow. Her own room was cream but all the soft furnishings were in deep shades of crimson and red. When the curtains were shut she felt as though she was an exotic princess reclining in her very own boudoir.

'Shall I get in touch with Michael?' Abby asked, looking at the way he was surveying her house and feeling appropriately invaded. 'I know where he is. I'm sure he'd love to come over and see you.'

Theo didn't rush into an answer. Instead he continued looking around him for a few more seconds before turning to her. He could have waited, could have seen his brother in a few days' time and found out what he needed to know, whether she had obeyed his instructions or not. In truth, he had no doubt that she would have. He had, after all, given her the choice of leaving with her reputation intact or leaving in disgrace at being exposed as a woman happy to be engaged to the one brother and make love to the other.

He had come to see her personally because in the past few weeks he had thought about her more than he cared to admit. It was a nuisance.

He looked at her now, staring up at him with those clear brown eyes, eyes that should have been matched with brown hair but were thrown into sharp, unusual relief by that exquisite thick vanilla-blonde hair.

'I wouldn't have come here if I had wanted to talk to my brother. No, I came here to see you.' He felt sudden annoyance and disgust with himself that he had made this trip to see this woman who clearly didn't want him in her house. 'I take it you're still in communication with my brother?' Beyond the small hall he could see the kitchen and he began walking towards it. 'You know where he is, right at this precise moment in time. This is not what I wanted to hear.' He had reached the kitchen. It was only a few paces from the front door, and he stopped. Stopped and stared, barely aware of her behind him. He filled up the doorway.

The kitchen was small but pretty. Grey speckled counter surfaces, pine units that looked cheap but functional, a very small oblong kitchen table that could sit four people provided they had no objections to being in very close physical contact with one another. Everything was on a very small scale. Small fridge freezer, small cooker, just sufficient units to store the bare essentials needed to make a kitchen actually work.

Theo, however, wasn't staring at the dimensions of the room. He was staring at the pictures on the fridge, magnets holding them up and at the little notice-board on the wall by the kitchen table. More pictures.

He stepped aside and Abby slipped past him, drawing in a deep breath as she took in the direction of his gaze. It was crazy. Jamie wasn't a secret!

'Interesting artwork,' Theo said, moving towards the fridge and inspecting the drawings tacked on it. One was some version of an underwater scene, another was of the family, which was comprised of a gigantic stick figure with lots of white hair and a much smaller one with a large smiley face, and then there were various attempts at writing.

Abby had no idea why she felt so nervous. She licked her lips and tried to relax. 'I think so.'

'Yours?' He removed the underwater scene and looked at it with exaggerated interest before holding it up for her to see.

'My son's.'

'You have a son. It's not…'

'No, it's not Michael's.'

The shutter had come down over her eyes. Theo watched and felt that flame of intense curiosity lick through him. He carefully adhered the picture back on to the fridge and then turned to her. 'Mind if I sit?'

'It's late.'

'Have you broken off the engagement? No, of course

you haven't. The ring's still on your finger.' Not only did she fail to deny it, but she didn't rush into any apology. His dark eyes hardened. 'You may think I'm playing games with you, but let me assure you that I'm not.'

'I won't let you attack me in my own house,' Abby told him, folding her arms protectively over her. God, she felt so nervous and so intimidated and, amongst all this, so hungrily drawn to the man sitting in her chair, in her kitchen, for all the world as though he had a stake there. Only seeing him there, in the flesh, made her recognise just how much he had been in her head and how disastrously easy it was for all those hidden feelings to spring back into life against all common sense and reason. They were raising their heads now, reminding her how treacherously good it had felt when he had kissed her, taken her in his arms, touched her breasts...

Abby closed her eyes briefly and then looked at him. 'Jamie wakes up easily. I don't want to have an argument with you here. This house has walls like paper.' Bring Jamie into the conversation, she thought, and remind herself about reality instead of letting herself float off on some pathetic whimsical cloud of nonsense.

'Ah. Jamie. I thought so.'

'What does that mean? That *you thought so*?'

'The handwriting on the piece of paper on the fridge, and those on the notice-board. He's learning how to write his name. How old is he?'

'Five.'

'What does he look like?'

'Why are you interested?'

'I'm curious. Why didn't you mention him before? To my mother? Our relatives? You had every opportunity.' His eyes narrowed on her pinkened face.

'I didn't think it was the right time...'

'Give me a clue as to what you think the right time *would* have been? Maybe sitting in a restaurant somewhere? My mother asking whether you had any little kiddies in tow? A natural question any prospective mother-in-law would pose to her son's fiancée?'

'You're not funny!' Anger made her voice rise a couple of decibels. Her blasted hair kept brushing her face and, without thinking, she flicked the hairband from her wrist, something she always kept handy, and roped it back into a ponytail.

'Maybe you decided that you could win Michael over to playing daddy to your little boy but breaking the news to the rest of us would be a more uphill task. Is that it? Build up to it in stages, maybe, rather than risk us all seeing the obvious.'

'And you're about to tell me *that obvious*, aren't you? Not that I can't guess where you're going!' Her small hands were bunched into fists and she was leaning forward, every nerve in her body stretched to breaking-point.

'It makes sense!' Theo thundered. He slammed his fist down on the table with such ferocity that Abby jumped. 'I wondered about you! You didn't seem like a money-minded gold-digger, but then I wasn't in possession of all the facts at the time, was I? How much do you earn?'

'How *much do I earn*? That's none of your business!'

'Enough to support yourself, I presume! With a little left over for small luxuries! But a child? Enough to support a child as well? I may not have children, but I know they are a commodity that doesn't come cheap. Is that why you decided that having a little financial help in that direction might be a good idea? And Michael would have been an easy target, not the sort of man to be put off by a child in the background. Did you string him along with some sob story? Make him feel sorry for you?'

'Children are not *commodities*!'

'Where is the boy's father? Does his maintenance not come up to scratch?'

'Stop it!' Abby shouted. 'How *dare* you walk into my house and start shouting at me? You insulted me when I was in Greece, when I was *on your terrain*, but *don't you dare* walk into *my* terrain and think you can continue doing the same thing!'

She stared at him, white-faced with anger and in the still silence it took a few seconds to register that he was no longer looking at her but beyond her, towards the door. She slowly turned round to find her son standing there, staring at them with bewilderment and fear. Mummies didn't shout. Ever. Abby had never shouted in front of him in her life before. She couldn't even remember ever shouting, not for years. Not until now. It was as if all the emotions she had carefully tidied away over the years had found some kind of nightmarish release and were now bursting out of their restraints. She was shaking when she stooped down to look at Jamie.

'Hi, kiddo. What are you doing up? You know you should be in bed. School tomorrow.'

'I heard shouting.' His eyes slipped past her to look warily at Theo. 'Who's that?'

'No one.'

'I am Theo, Michael's brother.'

Abby could feel him behind her, then she was aware of him stooping down next to her, the man who had accused her of sobbing her way into his brother's affections, playing on her status as a single mother to twist Michael into sympathising, into offering her marriage and his fortune as a way of protecting her. His voice was soft but he was still the same man who had admitted seeing children as *commodities*. Abby protectively pulled Jamie in to her and glared at Theo over her son's head. She was gently pressing him into the comfort of her shoulder, but already Jamie was wriggling, eager to continue his inventory of the stranger in his mother's kitchen. He managed to squirm free and proceeded to sit cross-legged on the floor, with Abby's hands loosely covering his chubby ones.

'You look like Uncle Michael. Doesn't he, Mummy?'

'I can see one or two differences,' Abby said through gritted teeth.

Theo felt his lips twitch. She looked like a small, frustrated, enraged angel. He had to remind himself that after his logical examination of the situation, after his concise conclusions about her behaviour and her motivations, she was anything but angelic, whatever the layout of her features.

'Can you?' Theo said innocently. 'People say we look very much alike. Aside from the small height difference.'

'People say adders look like garden snakes. Aside from the small difference in toxin levels.'

Theo did his utmost not to grin. 'I struggle to find the compliment in that,' he said gravely and was entranced to see the angel glare even more ferociously at him. She was positively throbbing! Like a steam engine that should have been going full pelt but was temporarily derailed by circumstances beyond its control, in this case the restraining presence of her son.

Jamie had brightened up at the mention of snakes and had now launched into a convoluted account of snakes he had seen at the zoo, which confusingly seemed to be tied in to a school book his teacher was reading to them in class about magic carpets. Theo didn't have a clue where the story was leading but he was enraptured by the childish enthusiasm and the striking similarity the boy had to his mother. The hair was a dirtier shade of blond but he had the same eyes and nose and mouth.

Who was the father? Where was he? Was he on the scene, maybe even still sleeping with her? That thought made him feel sick and he instantly thrust it away.

The angel had swivelled her son to face her and was now giving him a stern lecture on going to bed, at which point Theo was amused to find a process of bargaining kick off, with Jamie tentatively striking out for chocolate, the unspoken bribe being that some chocolate would see him happily heading back to his bed, and Abby forced to negotiate along liquid lines as an alternative, moving up from a glass of milk to finally settle on a carton of juice.

He stood up and edged back towards the table, watching silently as mother scooped up boy in one arm and efficiently located a carton of juice from the cupboard with her free hand. His presence was forgotten by both of them. She was entirely focused on her son, on getting him upstairs and Jamie was now absorbed in the fundamentals of trying to unstick the straw from the side of the carton.

Had Michael been drawn in by this? Theo wondered. He listened abstractedly to the sound of footsteps disappearing up the stairs. Had his brother found this charming sketch of mother and son just too difficult to resist? Add to the equation the fact that the mother in question had the face of an angel and a body which she denied him and had it been just too impossible to walk away? Something in the picture didn't make sense, but when he tried to analyse what that something was he found his mind wandering. Wandering to the look of her when she had been holding her son, to the way those slender arms could also be strong and supportive, to the way her brown eyes had been proudly assured as a mother and equally defensive. He clicked his tongue in frustration and dragged his mind back to the task at hand, which was to find out why she hadn't broken off the engagement and what she hoped to gain by temporarily thwarting him.

He had made them both a cup of coffee by the time Abby returned to the kitchen.

'You're still here,' she said, standing in the doorway, arms folded.

'You didn't really expect me to have left, did you?' Theo asked silkily. 'I've made you some coffee. Milk, no sugar. Is that how you take it?'

Abby didn't answer. Instead, she sat down on the chair opposite him, the furthest away from him, and sighed wearily. 'I can't fight with you any more,' she said, propping her chin in her hands and staring at him.

'I don't want a fight either, whatever you might think.'

'I know.' Abby gave him a watery smile. 'You just want me to clear out of your brother's life so that I don't get my greedy little paws on his millions.'

Theo flushed darkly. She was only saying what he had been thinking, after all, but put starkly like that it made him out to be the villain and her the sacrificial lamb. But she looked exhausted, that much was true. Rather than plunge headlong into another attack on her temerity in disobeying his orders to end her preposterous engagement, Theo decided that it wouldn't do any harm to slow the pace a bit. A clever negotiator knew that timing was the key thing. He sat back, cradling the cup in his hands, and looked at her lazily.

'You have a cute son.'

'Don't you mean a cute *commodity*?'

'I apologise for that. It was simply a mistake of speech.'

'Was it? Well, it doesn't matter anyway.' She sipped some of the coffee, which was surprisingly good. Or maybe she was surprisingly unsteady and anything hot would have tasted fine. She could feel those clever, searching eyes boring into her. The fluorescent light in the kitchen made everything stand out in sharp focus and right now Abby didn't need it. He was perceptive enough without the additional aid of bright lighting. She stood up, coffee in one hand.

'I'm going into the sitting room. I'm going to drink this coffee and then you are going to leave.' She didn't give him a chance to answer. Instead, she spun round and headed directly to the little room which was just off the hallway. The light had faded and she drew the curtains then retreated to the sofa, curling up at one end of it and watching warily as Theo took the plumply cushioned chair by the door.

He was only a few inches taller than his brother, but he seemed to drown out her little house in a way Michael never did. Maybe it was because there was nothing restful about him, even when he wasn't actually *doing* anything.

'I'll break off the engagement.' Abby was the first to break the silence and there was resignation and regret in her voice. The wretched engagement had been a foolish idea in the first place, even though it had served both their purposes admirably. She looked defiantly at the big, masculine figure on the chair and saw Theo nod imperceptibly.

'He is not the man for you,' he murmured.

'No, no maybe he isn't,' Abby said bitterly. There *was* no man for her. She had closed her heart off to them a long time ago. Only Theo had crept through an unseen chink and made her respond, but that had just been the response of a healthy young woman aching for a physical touch, something she had not even been aware of having missed. And through that chink she could feel all sorts of other things creeping, all sorts of questions raising their ugly heads, looking for answers. 'Maybe no one is. For me, I mean. It was stupid to think...' Damn and double damn! She could feel her eyes beginning to fill up, going past the point where she could rapidly blink the tears away.

Through the shiny mist of unwanted tears she was aware of Theo breaching the distance between them, coming to sit on the sofa by her, reaching forward, handing her something—a hankie. Abby took it gratefully and wiped her eyes, mumbling an embarrassed apology, not daring to look directly at him for fear of seeing his revulsion at this display of emotion. Maybe he would imagine that she was putting it on, trying to wrest some sympathy from him. It would be just like him to imagine the worst of her.

'Stop apologising,' Theo murmured. He brushed his thumb over one wayward tear struggling down her cheek and Abby shuddered, helplessly drawn to him and furiously aware that she shouldn't be.

'You should go now,' she whispered, looking down. 'You've heard what you came to hear and you have my word. About the engagement.'

'What did he do to you?'

'Michael? He didn't do anything to me...' Puzzled brown eyes met steady black ones and she knew instantly what he was referring to.

'Does he know that he has a son?'

'It's time for you to go.'

'You should let it go. Holding on to the past is a dangerous game. The past can be a cruel master.'

'How would *you* know?' Abby threw at him. 'You were born into privilege! Oh, don't tell me…you learnt from a young age the hardships of knowing that you could just snap your fingers and get anything you wanted! Poor Theo. Such misery to overcome!'

'Some might say that having your destiny worked out from the day of your birth was a pretty rough ride,' Theo said quietly, allowing himself the ridiculous luxury of confiding in someone else. Where had that come from? Baring his soul had never been something high on his list of priorities. In fact, it had never featured there at all. All that self-indulgent confessional nonsense was, as far as he was concerned, a Western disease. 'Michael may have had the freedom to do what he wanted, but as the heir to the empire I had no choice,' he continued shortly. 'Which isn't to say that I spent my life moaning about it.'

'I don't *moan* about my past,' Abby muttered. 'I've learnt from it.'

'What did he do to you?' Theo asked curiously. 'Do you still see him? You must, when he comes to take his son out.'

'He… He's never seen his son,' Abby blurted out. She watched Theo's expression harden into disbelief and the bitterness she had believed to have put to rest flooded her system like bile. 'Well, you have to understand that when a married man suddenly discovers that his mistress is pregnant it isn't exactly music to his ears…'

'You were involved with a married man?' Why, he wondered, did he feel so disappointed?

'Don't tell me it would surprise you if I was,' Abby said caustically, reading his mind. Then she sighed and drew her legs up so that she could rest her chin on her knees. 'I didn't know he was married when I got involved with him. I was nineteen and he was just a fantastically sexy man ten years older than me. Things were beautiful for eighteen months or so until I made the mistake of getting pregnant.'

'At which point your knight in shining armour revealed his feet of clay,' Theo filled in.

'He told me that he was married, that what we had had been nothing but a spot of fun, something to do in London during the week because he always returned to the Home Counties on the weekends to be with his wife and their two-year-old daughter. In fact, I wasn't even the only one! Although he was kind enough to tell me that I had been the only one to have stayed the course as long as I had. There. You wanted to know and now you do.' She sprang up and edged away from him. 'Now go. Before you tell me that I deserved what I got!'

Theo vaulted up but she was already rushing outside, rushing towards the front door.

He heard it before he had time to make it further than the sitting room door. Her sharp cry of pain followed by a muffled groan…

CHAPTER SEVEN

ABBY felt as though someone had decided to take a swing at her ankle with a hammer. How had it happened? One minute she was dashing to the front door as if the hounds of hell were at her heels, and the next minute she had flung open the door and taken one step, one small step and bang! Down she had gone, missing her footing on the shallow step down to the front path. The same shallow step she routinely warned Jamie to be very careful of.

Naturally Theo would have heard her cry out and she didn't bother to look up as she heard him cover the distance from the sitting room to the front door, where she was sitting inelegantly on the ground outside, clutching her throbbing ankle.

'What happened?' He knelt down to her level and Abby gave him a jaundiced look.

'What do you think?' she snapped. 'I tripped. But I'm fine.' She made a valiant effort to heave herself up and immediately collapsed back down.

'Don't be a fool.' Without waiting for a retort, Theo scooped her up and brought her back into the house, kicking the door shut with one foot, then making his way to the sitting room where he proceeded to gently deposit her on the chair. 'Right. Let's have a look.'

Abby didn't have to look to know that her foot was already beginning to swell. Instead, she stared ahead and tried to fight down the urge to blub like a baby from the pain. She only risked a glance down when she felt his fingers gently inspecting her foot. Her instinct was to yank the offending foot away but just the thought of moving it made her wince.

'Not good,' Theo said, looking up at her briefly. Well, it certainly made a change having him literally at her feet, but she was in too much pain to appreciate her own humour. Her fists were balled, fingernails digging into the soft flesh of her palms.

'Thank you for that opinion,' Abby said through gritted teeth, 'but, believe it or not, I had reached the same conclusion myself.'

'I'll get you some painkillers then we're going to have to take you to Casualty.'

'Have you forgotten the small matter of a five-year-old boy sleeping upstairs?'

'Is there anyone who could stay with him? A neighbour, maybe? Whoever looked after him when you were out in Greece playing the loving partner to my brother?'

Abby ignored the taunt tacked on at the end. 'I don't know any of my neighbours. At least not well enough to ask any of them to come and look after Jamie overnight, and Rebecca lives in the centre of Brighton. She stayed here for the week as a favour to me but she's not within easy travelling distance.' She grimaced. 'I really need some painkillers. They're on the kitchen counter.'

Theo stood up, frowning, and when he returned a couple of minutes later with a glass of water and two tablets he had worked out the only solution.

'We'll just have to wake your son up, in that case, and take him with us.'

'My foot can wait.' The hammering had subsided into nasty shooting daggerlike stabs instead. With any luck the tablets would take the edge off, enough for her to get some rest and then make her way to Casualty the following morning. She began telling him but he was already shaking his head before she had reached the end of her speech.

'This foot needs to be seen to *now*, tonight. If you can't or won't go to a doctor, then a doctor has to come to you.'

'Fat chance of any doctor doing a call out on a Sunday evening! The painkillers should help me get through the night…'

'The painkillers are designed for headache relief, Abby, not a possible broken ankle.'

'It's not broken!' Abby wailed. She couldn't afford to be immobile, not with a lively five-year-old needing to be taken to school and fed and watered and bathed and amused! Tears of frustration welled up in her eyes as a catalogue of impossible obstacles loomed in front of her. This was the final reckoning of the single mother with no convenient relatives close by and friends who were all young, free and single. Self-pity merged with frustration. Holding down a full-time job had meant that she had no social contact with any of the other mothers at the school. Jamie stayed until four, when she collected him. On the odd occasion when she had been unable to arrive on time his best friend's mother took him home with her, but she hardly knew the woman. They chatted politely enough and made arrangements for the children, but that was the extent of their acquaintance.

'What's the number of your surgery?'

Abby dully gave it to him. She knew it from memory, not that she had ever had to access that information in an emergency. She was too preoccupied with the ever increasing list of reasons why she couldn't have a broken ankle to be fully aware of Theo snapping open his mobile phone and dialling the number. Of course the surgery was shut but there was an emergency number given on the recorded message. The doctor on the end of the line didn't stand a chance of refusing to pay a home visit, not once Theo had swung into action. There was urgency in his voice, but also the unspoken assumption that Dr Hawford would not hesitate to abandon his bed on a Sunday evening and make his way to her house so that he could inspect her already swollen foot.

'Painkillers working yet?' he asked, snapping shut his phone and dragging the low stool by the television so that he could position it right next to her and sit down.

'Thank you for phoning the doctor,' Abby said. 'I'm sure you'll want to be on your way now. It's late and London isn't just around the corner.'

'Too true.' Theo flicked his hand out and glanced at his watch. 'After ten. No point heading back to London. I'll have to stay here.'

'*Here?*' Abby squeaked, horrified. 'You can't stay *here*! Have you forgotten about Jamie? And, besides, my house is too small! There are only two bedrooms and both of them are fully used! If you put your foot on the gas it shouldn't take too long to get back to London!'

'Are you advocating that I break the speed limit to accommodate you?'

'I'm telling you that you're not staying here!' She briefly forgot the horrendous pain in her foot under the even more oppressive thought of having Theo under her roof overnight. She had visions of him sharing her bathroom, shaving at her basin in the morning, using her towel to wrap around his body when he was through with his shower. She felt sick.

'I wasn't proposing to spend the night in your house,' he clarified. 'I was proposing that I stay with my brother.'

'You can't do that.' The words were out before her

brain had a chance of editing them. 'I mean you can't do that *without calling him first*. Michael keeps weird hours. You might show up to find he's not in and then you'll just be left kicking your heels outside his apartment for hours.'

'On a Sunday?' he asked mildly, puzzled at her immediate rejection of his idea. He looked at her flushed face narrowly. 'You're right. I wouldn't want to be left kicking my heels outside an empty apartment for hours. I'll call him now. He'll want to know about your little accident anyway, I'm sure.'

Before Abby had time to offer an opinion on this idea the wretched mobile phone was being flicked open again and this time her ears strained to hear every segment of the conversation.

She was only privy to one side of the conversation, but it wasn't difficult to hazard an intelligent guess as to what was being said on the other end of the line. Or even to picture Michael in the club, his phone glued to his ear, walking towards his office at the back so that his brother's voice didn't have to compete with the sound of voices and music.

There was a brief explanation of what Theo was doing in her house, which he managed to successfully waffle his way through with some phoney excuse about expecting to find Michael there. Abby almost snorted at this. Then there was a brief account of the ankle, tellingly lacking in all details as to how she had managed to trip in the first place.

'But now I'm here,' Theo said, 'it seems somewhat ridiculous to make my way back to London at this hour. I take it your apartment sleeps more than one?' Theo frowned at whatever response met that question, although she knew that Michael had expressed delight at having his brother stay with him. She had heard his exclamation from where she was sitting! Perhaps it had been that fractional hesitation before he responded. Too bad.

'Oh, and by the way,' she heard him say in the voice of someone wrapping up a conversation, 'so sorry to hear that the engagement is off…'

'How dare you?' Abby fumed, as soon as the phone was tucked back neatly into his pocket. '*How dare you?*' Her cheeks were bright with colour. This man was proving a far more effective painkiller than any tablet. Who had time for focusing on a minor thing like pain when her brain was fully occupied with searing fury?

'I just thought I would circumnavigate the possibility of you not sticking to your word. After all, you had weeks to do it yourself, but you somehow didn't seem to manage it. Funny, Michael didn't react quite as I had expected him to…' He fixed his amazing eyes on her flushed face.

'What do you mean?' Abby asked uneasily.

'He was silent for a few seconds, but then he immediately expressed regret. No shock, no surprise, no offer to rush over here to talk things through, which I might have expected from a man suddenly confronted with a bombshell.'

'You had no right to say anything.'

'You left me no choice. Why did my brother take the news so unquestioningly, do you imagine?' Something wasn't adding up. Nothing added up. All his presumptions made perfect sense in theory, but in practice it was like a puzzle missing a few key pieces.

'I…we…I hinted over the past few weeks that perhaps being engaged wasn't right for us…'

'Why didn't you mention that to me?'

'Because it was none of your business!' Abby flared.

She looked away, praying that the doctor would do something useful like pull up, and for once her prayers were answered because she heard the sound of a car pulling up to the house, followed by a door slamming and footsteps clicking up the path. Her body sagged in mute relief when the doorbell rang.

She had no doubt that Theo would have liked nothing better than to pursue the conversation until he had obtained one or two answers that at least made sense, but as it turned out he had no choice but to sigh with impatient frustration before disappearing to let the doctor in.

'Right.' Dr Hawford was a mild-mannered man in his early fifties, good with his patients and reassuringly efficient. 'Let's have a look, Miss Clinton.' He squatted by her foot and gently manipulated it, asking her to tell him when it hurt and how much, running through his standard questions in a quietly soothing voice.

In the background Theo hovered like a predator temporarily denied its prey. At least, that was how Abby felt.

'A class two sprain,' the doctor said, pushing himself up and then moving to sit on the sofa with his little black bag. 'You've done a good job of tearing some of your ligament fibres, hence the swelling and the pain. The good news is that there is no hospital intervention needed for a sprain such as this. The bad news is that you're going to be off your feet for a few days, possibly as long as a week.'

'I can't be off my feet for a few days, Doctor.'

'Have you informed your foot of that?' He looked at Theo. 'Fetch some ice, or something cold if there's no ice in the freezer. A packet of frozen peas will do nicely instead. It's important we try and get the swelling down. Now, my dear…' having dismissed Theo, he looked at

Abby not unsympathetically '…I know you've got a little boy but there is no way you are going to be able to carry out your normal duties for a few days, and if you try putting weight on this foot too soon you could do some quite severe damage that would have you out of action for far longer.'

'But…'

'Absolutely no room for manoeuvre, Abby. Now, I'm going to prescribe some anti-inflammatory drugs which will help with the pain and the swelling.' He pulled out his prescription sheet and Abby watched in numbed silence as he scribbled on it. 'You get your young man to fill this in first thing in the morning.'

'He's not my young man,' Abby said through gritted teeth just as Theo was walking back into the room with a bag of frozen vegetables in one hand and a clean tea towel in the other.

'And you might want to think about getting some strapping to fit over the injured ankle,' the doctor continued, looking at Theo from over the rims of his reading spectacles. 'Any good chemist will stock what you need. But, my dear—' he looked at Abby and stood up '—don't overuse any taping. Might feel comfortable but you don't want that ankle to become lazy! As soon as you can, probably tomorrow, you can start trying to exercise it. Which *does not mean applying it to the clutch and brake pedals of a car!*'

'I think I'm going to have to cancel my arrangements with Michael, don't you?' was the first thing Theo said once he had shown the doctor to the door and returned to the sitting room.

Abby just looked at him in miserable silence. 'I can manage,' she said eventually, something that was so patently untrue that Theo didn't bother to answer. Instead, he simply walked towards her and, ignoring her protests, picked her up.

'I'll lock up and turn off the lights after I've got you into bed.'

'You will do no such thing! I can manage perfectly well on my own!'

'As we all can when we can't walk.'

'Look—' Abby breathed in deeply and decided to go for the mature approach '—once you get me into bed I'll be able to manage just fine for myself and I can call Peter's mum first thing in the morning so that she can come and collect Jamie for school. It won't be a problem sorting out transport arrangements for him and I'm sure Rebecca wouldn't mind coming across some time tomorrow evening with some foodstuff. It's a bit of a trek for her, but she'll understand.' She could feel the muscled hardness of his torso against her and bit her lip nervously. 'I mean…'

'Which one is your bedroom?'

'The one on the right. Did you hear a word I just said?'

'Every word,' Theo said, shouldering open her bedroom door and somehow managing to switch on the light without dropping her. 'I just chose to ignore it because you must know as well as I do that you're talking rubbish.' He placed her on her bed, a luxurious double bed complete with feather mattress, which had been her one big extravagance when she had begun the task of furnishing her house. He then proceeded to straighten up so that he could stare down at her. 'You heard what the doctor said. No walking. Now, explain to me how you intend to sort your son out in the morning without getting off the bed. Unless you've mastered magic skills no one's capable of, then it just can't be done.' He shoved his hands in his pockets and waited for her to refute his baldly logical statement. 'Which leaves me no option but to stay here. Especially now that you and Michael are no longer an item. I mean...' Out came the mobile phone again. Abby was beginning to heartily hate the sight of the thing. 'It wouldn't really do for the heartbroken fiancé to be called to do nightly duty with the woman who let him down, would it?' This time his conversation with his brother was brief. A two-minute imparting of information, no more. 'Nope. No offer to try and patch things up by rushing over to comfort you in your moment of need. Disappointed?'

'Of course Michael can't rush over here and babysit me,' Abby muttered sourly. 'He works weird hours.'

'Oh, but I thought that he might just find the wellbeing of his woman more important than supervising a kitchen in a restaurant. After all, overseeing onion chopping and pastry preparation can't be as important, surely, as coming here to visit you, especially when he's suddenly found himself cast out into the cold without so much as a formal warning of intent.'

'That was *your* fault. You had no right to tell him that I had broken off the engagement. I would have told him myself.'

Theo didn't bother to answer. Instead he strolled over to her chest of drawers and pulled open the first one. Abby gave a strangled squeak of horror.

'You need to change,' he said without turning around. 'And I'm going to have to help you.'

'Help me? *Help me? Change?*' She squirmed up the bed and her ankle protested with rage at the sudden movement.

'There. Is this what you sleep in?' He turned round and dangled her oversized T-shirt from one finger. 'I've looked but I can't spot anything else that could be passed as nightwear unless your negligées and French knickers are stashed away somewhere else?' He grinned and the urge to throw something at him was so strong that she actually snarled under her breath.

'I can get it on myself!' She watched as he continued to dangle the item in front of her.

'I'll need to help you with those jogging things you've got on.'

'I'm not an invalid.'

'You heard what the doctor said. No pressure on the ankle or risk the consequences. Now, why don't you start behaving like a good little girl and let me help you?'

He moved towards her and Abby heaved a deep sigh of resignation. To be helpless was bad enough but to be at the mercy of this man was almost unbearable. And he was in a stunningly cheerful mood. She knew why. He had achieved what he had come to do. Not content to trust her to obey his instructions and remove herself from his brother, he had simply taken matters into his own hands and done it for her. She doubted whether he had paused to consider the fallout of his actions. He had simply done what he did best, which was to bypass all obstacles and get to the destination by the shortest route possible. Feelings were minor technicalities that he had no time for. What if theirs had been a *real* engagement? Abby fretted. How would Michael have been feeling now? In all events, she would have to telephone him as soon as she could and explain what had happened.

In the meantime…

She gritted her teeth and then closed her eyes when Theo slowly and gently extricated her from the trousers. Then he manoeuvred her under the quilt and neatly placed the T-shirt next to her.

'I'm doing you both a favour,' he murmured gently

and Abby opened her eyes and looked at him with deep scepticism. 'The thought of all that money must have seemed tempting, especially when you have all those expenses associated with bringing up a child, but can you truthfully say that you would have been happy living with someone you had no feelings for?'

'I do happen to have a lot of feelings for Michael.'

Strangely enough, that was not what Theo wanted to hear. His mouth tightened as he sat on the bed next to her. 'You were badly hurt once. Maybe you do have feelings for Michael, but maybe they're the wrong kind of feelings.' He looked at her thoughtfully. 'I may have been wrong about you,' he mused slowly. 'I assumed that you were little more than a common gold-digger, out to get your sweaty little hands on my brother's money, whatever it took. But, thinking back on it, you didn't really fit the image. Not that there *is* a gold standard for the gold-digger. They come in all shapes and sizes!' His dark eyes roved over her face until Abby felt herself begin to go warm under the lazy scrutiny. But something inside her unfolded with pleasure at the thought that he was no longer writing her off as the lowest of the low. She told herself that she couldn't care less what the man thought of her, but that didn't stop the little bubble of pleasure, even though her face remained coolly impassive.

'Should I be pleased that you've changed your mind? When you've taken matters into your own hands and told Michael that I no longer wanted to...' she couldn't bring herself to say the word *marry* '...to be his fiancée? Leaving him to think that I was discussing my personal affairs with *you* before I had discussed them with *him*?'

'Regrettable, I admit.'

'And that's all you have to say about it?' She stoked

herself up to some healthy anger because he was leaning over her now, hands squarely placed on either side of her prone body, which was quivering with shameful awareness. 'You are the most obnoxious...'

'I know. I think you've told me that before. But I still make you feel things my brother never did and never could. Admit it. I don't know whether you would have gone ahead with a wedding if I hadn't come along, but I did and I think we both know that I've done you a favour.'

'How can you *sit there* and calmly justify your behaviour?'

'It's all in the name of truth,' Theo drawled. 'And I am honest enough to admit when I have made a mistake. Of course, you were marrying Michael for the wrong reasons, but the intent was not quite as straightforward as I originally thought. You are a single mother with a deep mistrust of the opposite sex. Michael was the unthreatening protector, the safe haven. No surge of emotions to deal with but then...no chemistry either. It would have been a match made in hell.'

Abby watched the dark, devilishly sexy face with reluctant fascination. So much right and so much wrong. 'I don't need any surge of emotions,' she heard herself say. 'I had those once and they didn't do me any good.'

'Wrong man,' Theo murmured. In the dim lighting the unsteady rise and fall of her breasts was mesmerising. The vision that had been haunting him for weeks rose into his head with disturbing clarity, the memory of those breasts and the feel of them under his hands, the taste of them. He had to get out of this room and quick or he would end up behaving like a sad besotted fool, happy to take advantage of a woman who literally couldn't run away from him. Sad he had never been and besotted…well, the word was simply not part of his vocabulary. He pulled back and stood up, quickly spinning round on his heel to hide the betraying bulge of his erection.

'I'll need a sheet,' he said abruptly, only turning round to face her when he was confident that his body was once more under control. 'I can sleep downstairs on the sofa. If you leave the bedroom door open and I leave the sitting room door open, I should be able to hear you if you call out for anything.'

'There's no need…'

'There's every need.' Theo's voice was harsh. 'It's my fault you took that fall in the first place and it's my responsibility to make sure that you don't do any further damage by trying to put weight on the foot.'

'How is it *your fault*?' She had visions of him creeping up the stairs in the middle of the night to check on her, seeing her in all her sleeping vulnerability.

'If you hadn't been running away from me, you would never have tripped on that step down. If you ended up doing untold damage to your foot because I took off now, I would carry the weight of it on my mind for the rest of my life.'

It made it easier to think that his motives were entirely selfish. Abby could breathe a sigh of relief at that because it fitted the category she was increasingly desperate to fit him into. The minute he climbed out of his neatly labelled box, she seemed to lose control of the steering wheel, as she had just then, when he had been sitting there on the bed, being perfectly controlled and rational and still managing to send every pulse in her body racing wildly out of control.

'And we can't have that, can we?' she said, coolly sarcastic. 'There are sheets in the airing cupboard on the landing and a couple of spare pillows as well. I always have those in case Jamie wants a friend over for the night.'

'Right. And his school is…?'

'I can get him to walk to school with one of the mums.'

'I'll take him.' The expression in his eyes didn't encourage her to think that a debate was on the agenda, and she briefly gave him directions. All along, she had been thinking about herself, thinking about the nightmare of having him around, even for one night, and what that did to her fragile equilibrium. She hadn't spared a thought for the fact that he was a high-powered businessman and this unforeseen incident must have been the last thing he would have expected or wanted, but he had stayed because she was physically incapable of doing all the things she had vehemently told him she could do.

'Thank you,' Abby said simply. 'I know you're staying here tonight because you feel obliged to, but I'm very…grateful anyway.'

'There's no need to act as though the words are being torn out of you.' He gave her a crooked smile. 'Didn't you know that there's nothing a man likes better than a woman he feels the need to protect?'

And he would make any woman the best protector was the first thing that flashed through her head. Before she acknowledged that he was simply being as courteous about the inconvenience as he could. She smiled faintly at him. 'I'll remember that when I'm yelling for you at two in the morning because I need another dose of painkillers.' And he wouldn't object. Even with her, someone he disliked, whatever he said about not believing her to be the person he had first thought. Abby felt a sudden shift in her thinking. She had once imagined Oliver to be like that, but time had proved her wrong. He had been monstrously selfish and exploitative, but Theo...

She didn't want to go there, though. Instead, she waited until he had left the room, then she reached for the phone by her bed and dialled Michael's mobile number. He had amazing stamina and was in wicked form when he recognised her voice.

'He thought you took our broken engagement very well,' Abby said, cutting him off in mid speculation about his brother spending the night in her house. 'So, just to let you know, I told him that we had discussed the possibility that marriage might not be the ideal route for us to take.'

'I'll be suitably heartbroken.'

'Michael...you could always come clean.'

'I prefer to play the heartbroken ex-fiancé, thanks.' He laughed but changed the subject, asking her about her foot, for details of how it had happened, chipping in with comments. Then, obviously in no particular rush despite the lateness of the hour, he gave her a long description of the jazz band who had played at his night club.

'I can pop in over the next few days and make sure that you and Jamie have enough to eat,' he concluded.

'Your idea of buying food doesn't cater sufficiently for someone who can't make it down the stairs to cook or for a five-year-old palate, come to think of it.'

'I'll pop in anyway. Who's going to be available while you're off the pegs? Will you be able to get Rebecca over to help out?'

Not a chance, thought Abby. Her indebtedness to one person was already bad enough without extending it to anyone else. Whatever the doctor said, she was pretty sure that she could hobble to the kitchen and, just so long as Jamie was content with the television set and a couple of board games, she would be fine. She was certain of it. What was the point of two legs if you couldn't make use of the good one when the other one was out of action? But she knew that if she mentioned any such thing Michael would arrange for someone to come and take over the responsibility of her house for a few days. That, she thought drily, was the one thing his privileged background had granted him. He was always confidently sure that he could achieve anything. When she had first met him, she had assumed the trait came from a willingness to take a risk and, yes, he had taken risks, but now she knew that maybe he had always been aware of the fact that if he fell he would have fallen on a cushion. Not quite the same as a concrete floor.

She hurriedly assured him that she had everything in hand and was even quicker to inform him that his brother would be leaving first thing in the morning.

Which didn't seem to be the case when she surfaced to sunlight making its way weakly through her curtains and a polite knocking on her door, which was a few inches ajar.

Theo Toyas didn't look like a man suitably kitted out for heading back to his fast track in London. Abby struggled up a little further, biting back the sharp reminder of yesterday's little fall which her foot was issuing, and glanced at her watch. Ten-thirty! She yelped.

'You were dead to the world.' He strolled towards her, two small white tablets in one hand, a glass of water in the other. 'So I didn't wake you and I made sure that Jamie was as quiet as a mouse. He rather enjoyed the game.'

'You shouldn't have let me lie in!' Abby threw aside the quilt but the simple act of trying to swing her legs out of bed made her cry out in pain.

'No. I should have shaken you till you got up and then insisted you come downstairs!' He handed her the pills and, as she swallowed them, she listened as he filled in the gaps of her missing hours. While she had been cheerfully sleeping he had been up since six, had handled Jamie, taken him to school and on the way back had stopped off to buy himself a change of clothes and some food. Oh, and of course, collect her prescription.

'Now—' he sat on the bed, as sexy as hell in a short-sleeved striped cotton shirt and a pair of light trousers '—I'll help you to the bathroom. Then some breakfast. I'll carry you downstairs. Unless you'd like me to bring you it on a tray?'

Abby was aghast. This did not look like a man on the verge of vacating her premises. This looked like a man taking his responsibilities a little too seriously for her liking. And why did he have to look so damned *good*? She felt the soft hang of her breasts brushing the T-shirt, felt her nipples stiffening, and scowled at him.

'I'm sorry I messed up your night, but I'm not going to mess up your day. Don't you have to return to London? For meetings? Michael said that you hardly ever had a minute to spare when you came over here.'

'Actually, I *am* rather busy at the moment, but that's the joy of this modern life we now live. Have work can travel. Fortunately I automatically slung my laptop in the car with me when I drove from London, so I'm more than capable of keeping a tab on what's going on from here. I've had to cancel a couple of meetings, but I have people who are primed to slip into place whenever I can't make something.' He shot her a wry smile that sent tingles racing up and down her spine. 'I pay them enough. Now and again they need to justify their hefty salaries.'

'But…'

'I'll run a bath.' He left her floundering in what felt like a sudden onset of quicksand under her feet and was back before she could resign herself to the inevitable.

'Just for the day, then,' she said as he lifted her smoothly from the bed and carried her to the bathroom, turning her sideways through the door so that her foot was protected.

'If you say so,' Theo murmured agreeably. He could feel her warm and vulnerable in his arms, could hear the machinations of her brain as she dealt with his presence, was aware of the rapid beating of her heart. He felt like a boy of eighteen again, invigorated, challenged and prey to runaway emotions…

CHAPTER EIGHT

THE woman was a bag of contradictions.

He stared at the screen of his laptop computer, which he had set up on the kitchen table, making damned sure that the leads connecting it were well out of harm's way. His mind, however, was not focused on the emails blinking at him. For once, his formidable mind, which had been meticulously trained to concentrate on work in whatever place in which it presented itself, was wandering.

With an impatient grunt he stood up and wasted time making himself a cup of coffee while he wondered what she was doing in the sitting room. For someone who had been prepared to sell herself into a loveless marriage in an attempt to provide financial stability for her child she had been remarkably prudish when it came to having him help her with the bath. In fact, she had locked him out and done it herself, even if it *had* taken five times longer than necessary, a minor fact which he had pointed out several times through the closed door with increasing impatience. She had only brought herself to ask for his help when it came to manoeuvring herself downstairs, and even then she had refused to be carried, insisting on hobbling the best she could and tartly reminding him of the doctor's orders about making sure the foot started receiving some exercise. He had only agreed because the swelling had reduced and the painkillers were efficient.

This evening Michael would be coming round to visit, taking time out of his hectic schedule to cluck around the

woman who had dumped him. It didn't make sense. Theo
had never been dumped by a woman but he was damned
sure that if he had been the last thing he would have
wanted to do was clap eyes on the perpetrator, never
mind socialise with her over a civilised cup of tea. The
whole business was mystifying and Theo abhorred mys-
teries. He eyed the laptop and, with a sudden burst of
decision, tipped his coffee into the sink, snatched up the
computer and headed for the sitting room.

Abby was on the sofa, her legs stretched out in front
of her, the injured one slightly raised on a cushion. She
had used the tape he had purchased to wrap it herself and
he resisted the temptation to tell her that he could have
done a better job if she had dropped her pride and asked
him to.

Her face was soft and flushed as she looked up at him
from her book. Her hair had been neatly tied back into
braids and she was back to being the fragile child-woman
he had first clapped eyes on in Greece, stepping out of
the taxi and looking around her with an air of open won-
derment.

'Yes?' she asked, raising her eyebrows in a question.
'Do you want something?'

'Aren't you bored sitting in here by yourself, reading?
Would you like me to fetch you the remote control for
the television?' He dumped his laptop on the table by the
sofa and began walking round the room restlessly, pausing by the windows to peer outside at the little back garden with its collection of plastic toys neatly stacked away
to one side of the gravelled patio.

'I wish you'd stop prowling, Theo. It makes me feel
tired.'

Theo stopped and turned around to look at her. 'How
can you feel tired looking at someone?'

'I know you're feeling cooped up being here and I've already told you that you're free to leave. I'm managing just fine on my own. In fact, the swelling's all but gone and I can function. Not very quickly, but then I'm in no rush at this particular moment.'

'I'm staying until your foot's completely healed.'

'*Completely healed?*' Abby's mouth dropped open in shock. 'I thought you were leaving tonight.'

'Would that be conveniently before my brother arrives?'

'Why would I want you to leave before Michael comes?'

'Maybe you're afraid that I might ask him one or two pointed questions…?' He knew that he was angling for an argument and he knew why. He was jealous of his brother! There was no longer any engagement, but it irked him that there was still that warmth between them. He couldn't understand why that was the case but the nasty suspicion that maybe he had made a mistake in doing what he had known he had to do, for the sake of protecting his brother, lingered somewhere at the back of his mind. Maybe friendship without sex had been the perfect basis for a permanent relationship. Sex, after all, was transitory. How many times had *he* made love to a woman, had a full and passionate relationship with her, knowing all the while that the relationship was destined to end? 'Anyway, that's beside the point. You still haven't answered my question. Are you bored?'

'No, of course I'm not bored.' Abby gazed past the imposing figure by the window to where a light drizzle was threatening to turn into something more substantial. After a prolonged period of fine weather, the English sun was now doing what it did best, namely go into hiding. The forecast for the next few days was dismal. 'It's a perfect day to be laid up at home with a dodgy foot,' she said wistfully. 'Maybe if it was sunny I would be itching to be outside, doing something useful in the garden, but in weather like this it's wonderful being indoors.'

It was the most she had said to him all morning. Theo abandoned all thoughts of work, at least for the moment. He pushed himself away from the window and took up a position on the chair facing her, stretching out his long legs in front of him.

'Indoors doing nothing.'

'I'm reading.' Abby held up the book for him to see the boldly emblazoned title of a crime novel. 'I don't get enough time to read. I've been reading this for nearly six months and I'm only halfway through. In case you hadn't noticed, time rushes past at a frantic rate the minute kids are involved in the equation.'

'Yes, I *had* noticed, as a matter of fact,' Theo said dryly.

'Jamie wasn't too much trouble, was he?'

'He was very well behaved. Actually, I think he enjoyed having me around.'

'He enjoyed having *a man* around,' Abby corrected quickly. Gut instinct warned her that it would be a fatal error to slot Theo Toyas into the role of domesticated twenty-first century man. 'He's getting to an age when he's interested in cars and football and he's envious of his little friends who have fathers to share those interests with him.'

'Michael has never been interested in cars and football,' Theo felt constrained to point out. 'He might have been a male presence and a good meal ticket, but that would have been about it.'

'That's not why...'

'No? Tell me why then…' Theo interrupted her out-burst quick as a flash.

'You're right. Michael isn't much into cars or football. Well, at least not the football. He drives a very nice Porsche, which Jamie insists on sitting in every time he comes over.'

It hadn't escaped his notice that she had avoided his very pointed question, but he let it go. 'I don't suppose you have a lot of free time,' he conceded. 'You must have known what life would have been like with a baby. Did you ever contemplate…?'

'Getting rid of it? No, never! I wanted this baby the minute I knew I was pregnant. Maybe terminating a preg-nancy is something that works for other people, but it would never, ever have worked for me and I would never have contemplated it!'

'Whoa! It was just a question!'

'Well, would *you* ever think of asking your girlfriend or partner or wife to terminate a pregnancy because it didn't suit you?'

'No, of course I wouldn't. I would just make damned sure that the situation never arose in the first place. That's the beauty of contraception, isn't it? It allows a man to take control of his own virility.'

The direction of their conversation suddenly had Abby becoming a little too aware of a certain man's virility and she lowered her eyes. 'Anyway, I'm not bored. I like the sound of the rain outside and I find it very relaxing doing nothing. You should try it yourself some day.' She was rewarded with a smile of such dazzling amusement that her breath caught in her throat.

'I think that's what I'm doing at the moment,' he com-mented. When she turned her head like that her neck looked so delicate and vulnerable. His desire to go up to her, kneel alongside the sofa and brush back some of those loose strands of pale hair, was so overpowering that he had to clench his fists on the thought.

'You've brought your computer in with you.'

'But I've only glanced at it this morning and it's now…nearly midday…a personal record for me…'

Abby felt herself soften at the admission and she racked her brains to think of something prosaic to say that would dilute the sudden intimacy of their conversation.

'Well, you'd better get started,' she joked lightly, 'or else you might find you get used to doing nothing.'

'Oh, but I haven't quite been idle, have I?' Dark eyes narrowed wickedly on her face. 'I've been waiting on you hand and foot…'

'I never asked you to!'

'You can be extremely predictable in your responses…'

'Which is good,' Abby tossed back at him. 'Predictability is nice. I like that trait in a person.' Her immobility was beginning to get to her. She couldn't dodge his conversation nor could she physically walk away from it.

'Do you?' Theo murmured, then he sighed elaborately. 'Well, much as I would love to carry on sitting here and chatting away the remainder of the morning, I can't avoid work indefinitely.'

'No!'

'Which brings me to the reason I barged in on you in the first place, disturbing your peaceful, solitary interlude…'

'Yes…?' Abby looked at him warily.

'As I haven't been able to physically get into the office today…'

'Which wasn't *technically* my fault…'

'And will most likely not be going in tomorrow either…'

Abby took a few seconds to digest the sinking inevitability of that statement and only caught on to the rest of what he was saying when he had completed his sentence and was watching her, waiting for her input. Even then she had to reconstruct his words in her head before she grasped the meaning.

'You want me to *work for you*?'

'Just while I'm here. I have a number of things to dictate and my typing tends to involve two fingers and a great deal of wasted time.' He leant towards the table, picked up the computer and strolled over to where she was sitting. 'I think the kitchen table might get a little uncomfortable after a while. Here. You can rest it on your lap and as soon as you think it's beginning to feel a little awkward, just tell me.'

He settled the slim gadget on her lap and Abby's teeth snapped together as his fingers brushed against the fleecy cotton of her track pants.

'You know how to use one of these things, I take it…?'

'Yes, of course I do! But I'm really not sure I'm up to your standard of expectations.'

'You don't know what my standards of expectations are,' Theo pointed out, moving behind her and then leaning down so that he could manipulate the keyboard from behind. 'Is this okay for you? Tell me if the pressure of it on your foot is too much, won't you.' She must have washed her hair. It smelled of mint and eucalyptus. Fresh and clean. Like all true blondes, even the roots of her hair were fair. He surfaced to realise that she was asking him something about which files he needed to access.

Theo reached over her shoulder and moved the icon to

open the relevant box. Her fingers, doodling invisible patterns on the sides of the computer, were long and slender. He had a powerful image of those long slender fingers stroking him and he felt himself harden in immediate response to the mental image.

'Will you miss him?' he murmured, and Abby inclined her head with a little start at his question. His utterly irrelevant question. She felt her heart skip a beat, then begin to thud inside her.

'Miss who?'

'My brother. No engagement, no Michael. Will you miss him?' His breath gently blew strands of hair that tickled his face, but he didn't straighten up. He liked leaning over her like this, breathing her in, waiting for her reply. He could feel her tension. It was there in the stillness of her body. Her fingers were no longer doodling.

'Michael and I will always see one another.' Abby cleared her throat and tried hard to pretend that the big man behind her wasn't making every nerve in her body unravel in jittery awareness. Why was he standing so close to her, breathing over her? She couldn't think properly when he was this close. Her head felt as though it was stuffed with cotton wool. The fact that she had managed to speak at all was something of an achievement, as far as she was concerned, because her vocal cords seemed to be undergoing some weird drying up process.

'We're friends,' she said, stumbling over her words, 'and you don't just deposit friends by the wayside when they no longer suit you.'

Theo pulled back but, instead of walking away, he swooped round so that he was squatting by the side of her. 'It's not just a friendship thing, though, is it? It was a bit more than that. You might think that there would be some bad feeling between the two of you over a bro-ken engagement. Even if the relationship was never... shall we say, consummated?'

'Perhaps we should leave this for the moment and get on with the work,' Abby mumbled, reddening. 'I'm not a PA. I know a bit about computers but...' Those fabulous eyes staring at her made her feel uncomfortable. She almost squirmed in the chair. 'And anyway, I don't know how long I can remain here without moving. My foot's beginning to feel a little stiff...'

'Is it?' Immediately he was all concern. 'Maybe an ice-pack will do some good.' Before she could refuse any such offer of assistance, he was on his feet and heading out towards the kitchen. It gave her approximately three minutes of blissful relief before he was back in the sitting room. He had rigged up a strong plastic bag with ice inside and he proceeded to gently place it on her foot. The thing was freezing!

'It'll help,' Theo said, sensing her reaction without having to look at her. 'And I'll only leave it on for five minutes. You paint your toenails.'

'Lots of women do.'

'And so do some men.' Theo looked up and gave her a wicked smile. 'Paint their women's toenails, that is... Has a man ever done that for you?'

'No, of course not!' Abby spluttered, utterly at his mercy as he continued to manoeuvre the ice-pack around her foot.

'You sound horrified. Why? It's a very sensual thing to do.'

'My foot feels a lot better now, thank you,' she squeaked.

'Looks a lot better.' He removed the ice-pack and gave it a professional, measuring look. 'Right. Back in a minute. Don't go away!' He vaulted to his feet, ice-pack in hand, disappeared, only to return moments later with a pot in his hand. 'Cream,' he said, holding it up. 'I noticed you had some in the bathroom. Inertia is very bad for the circulation,' he carried on, opening the pot. 'Did you know that?'

'Maybe if you're bedbound for weeks,' Abby contributed desperately. 'But I've been off my feet for less than a day! I don't think my circulation is going to be affected. What are you doing?'

She knew exactly what he intended doing but her body still reacted with hot shock when he slid his fingers over her good foot and began massaging the thick cream into it, doing a very thorough job while keeping up a running commentary on the miracles of massage for easing away aches, pains, stress and, naturally, the non-existent circulation problem he claimed she was having.

'Relax,' he told her. 'I can feel your tension.'

'What do you expect?' But his hands were horribly relaxing and she gradually felt herself begin to enjoy the movement of his fingers between her toes, along the sides of her foot, against her heel. She leant back against the sofa, curving into the puffy cushion, and half-closed her eyes. His hands on her foot, working her ankle and calf, were magical. She pictured him painting the toenails of a woman, some voluptuous Greek goddess. She imagined he would make a meal of something like that, taking his time, turning it into a slow, languorous part of his foreplay. She felt herself soften inside at the thought and abruptly opened her eyes to see his dark head, still down-bent as he concentrated on what he was doing. And doing so well.

'That was very nice,' she said crisply.

'*Nice?* I never liked that word.'

'I'm ready for some hard work now.' Abby ignored his attempt to prolong a conversation she didn't feel capable of dealing with. She struggled into a semi-sitting position, which was hardly satisfactory, and Theo obligingly pulled the central coffee table closer to her so that she could swivel into an upright position. Of course, she had to allow him to manoeuvre her foot on to the table. More touching. *Innocent touching*, she reminded herself. Just like the foot was *innocent touching*.

'You know which program to log into?'

When she nodded he proceeded, thankfully, to give her concise instructions on what to do, and he kept a safe distance. Never had she felt so grateful for the safe haven of having to stare at a computer screen.

He dictated exactly as she had known he would. Word perfect, without the need to ponder over what he intended to say. It was one-thirty by the time he broke off and told her that she had to have something to eat.

'I'll take you out,' he announced, forestalling her objection with his hand. 'I'll make sure it's a pub and I'll park outside so you'll only have a short walk in leaning against me.'

'You don't know anywhere here. Really, this isn't a very good idea...'

'Why not? It solves the problem of you having to eat my food.'

'But...' But all this time in his company frightened her. But she didn't want to see these sides of him that she couldn't categorise and immediately dislike. But the way he touched her made the hairs on the back of her neck stand on end. A thousand buts that she couldn't put into words. 'But you need to get back to your own life in London...I mean, you really don't *owe* me all this attention! I'm nothing but a gold-digger. Have you for-gotten?'

'I made assumptions and I've revised them.' Theo looked at her in silence for a few moments. Even his silence made her skin prickle. 'Are you scared of being in my company?' he asked softly, and Abby rushed in with a hot denial of any such thing.

'Good. Then where's the problem?'

Which meant that twenty five minutes later they were sitting at a corner table in a very chic French restaurant. He had located it on his little hand-held device, which apparently did a very good job of supplying lists of highly regarded restaurants and was invaluable for him, bearing in mind the amount of time he spent in London. Which led to the inevitable questions about where he stayed when he was in London, whether he found his nomadic lifestyle tiring, whether he missed his mother country when he was away. Harmless questions that met with amusing replies that kept her thoroughly invigorated for the duration of the drive and throughout the superb meal. The one-dimensional cut-out figure she had as-sumed him to be when she had first encountered him was rapidly turning into a three-dimension flesh and blood man, and one who was sharp, witty, urbane and nothing, she told herself weakly, like the kind of man who should be interesting her.

'Now, I suggest we collect Jamie on the way back,' he told her, when he was paying the bill. Abby realised, disconcerted, that the time had disappeared.

'What about your work?' she asked. 'Once Jamie's home there's no chance of getting anything done.'

'Then I suppose we'll have to pick it up later.' He stood up and helped her to her feet. She had kept on the shirt she had been wearing in the house, but had managed to change into a skirt, which made her feel a great deal less constrained. 'Or maybe,' he murmured, easing her into his car, 'even tomorrow.'

So now another day had been tacked on. Worse, her desire to see the back of him was not what she would have wanted. Instead, a certain amount of pleasure had crept in at the thought of having him around for one more day. *Where had that come from?* She uneasily told herself that it was simple gratitude at his generosity in staying with her when there was no need. It was difficult not to have *some* warm feelings towards a person who had put himself out.

And then there was no opportunity to think more about it because Jamie was in the car, gabbling away about what he had done, producing pictures he had drawn like a magician drawing rabbits from a hat, asking his usual relentless blend of practical questions and ridiculous ones that always made Abby smile.

'Where does he get all that energy from?' Theo asked at one point and Abby grinned at him. She was having a delightfully easy ride due to her foot and was more than happy to watch how Theo coped with a child. Quite differently, she noted, from Michael. Whereas Michael was always happy to do sedentary things, like playing with Lego and building puzzles, Theo's solution to the problem involved kicking a ball in the garden, pretending not to hear her advice about windows and neighbours' gardens, then there was a ride in his car to the local fast food burger joint, which involved some token lip service paid to her concerns about junk food, and later a bath which, from where she was reclining in front of her book, was an adventure in water rather than a functional clean.

There was something to be said for a vigorous approach to childminding, however. By seven, Jamie's eyes were closing and she was halfway through a story when he nodded off completely and was taken upstairs by Theo.

'Have you had fun?' Abby asked when he re-appeared five minutes later and sprawled wearily down on the chair. Theo looked at her through half-closed eyes and thought that he hadn't experienced such simple fun for a very long time. His very adult fun was measured, sophisticated and highly costly.

'I've cancelled Michael,' he said, avoiding the question. 'I told him that you weren't quite up to visitors yet.'

'You said...*what*?'

'You heard me,' he drawled. 'I will see my brother before I leave and, since you two obviously have a friendship beyond my simple comprehension, you can see him any time you want. Just not tonight.'

'And you did that without consulting me?'

'Correct. Tell me what you want to eat for dinner. I can do my best with pasta but anything more complex might be inedible. Michael, I'm afraid, inherited all the culinary genes.'

'You can't just...just...cancel my arrangements without asking me first!'

'I already have.' He looked at her calmly while she spluttered herself into resignation.

'It would have been nice...I would have thought that you might have *wanted* to see your brother! It's hardly as though you two are in constant touch! Michael would have been horribly offended...I need to call him, explain that it wasn't my idea...'

'You don't have to explain anything to Michael.' Theo could feel his temper beginning to unravel. What the hell was going on here and why did he get the feeling that he wasn't completely in the picture? 'And why are you so concerned about what my brother thinks? Does he have something over you? Are you afraid of him for some reason?' Black eyes narrowed on her face and Abby looked at him with genuine astonishment.

'How could I ever be afraid of your brother? He's the kindest person I've ever met!'

'Then he'll understand why you need to rest,' Theo grated.

The way he was looking at her sent a thrill of gut-wrenching excitement through her and the latent aggression in his voice was sending her messages which her brain struggled to decipher. When he took a couple of steps towards her, her heart began to beat quicker. She licked her lips nervously and stared at him, quite unable to tear her eyes away from his staggering masculinity.

'Besides...' his voice was a thick, husky murmur, intensely sexy, intensely destabilising '...maybe it's a good thing my brother isn't going to be around tonight. He might be the good sport who took his broken engagement on the chin but how would he feel about the atmosphere between us?'

'What atmosphere?' One small part of her wanted to burst into hysterical laughter at the response Michael would have, the last response Theo would have expected. The greater part of her was trying hard to grapple with what was unravelling in front of her and with the steady thump of desire that was increasing in her by the second.

'You know what atmosphere.' Theo was now standing right over her, looking down, noticing with satisfaction the quickening of her chest as she nervously gulped in air. He reached down and delicately stroked her forearm with his finger. He could almost hear her sigh and it was a turn-on beyond his wildest imaginings. 'It was there in Greece,' he murmured, giving her no time to recover from what he was saying. He dropped to his knees and bent to kiss the delicate jut of her collarbone.

Abby shivered and managed to utter a weak *'No.'*

'Yes,' he said. 'You want me in a way you couldn't possibly ever want my brother. I proved that once and now I want more…'

'You can't…'

'Because you don't want it? Because you don't want *me*? Why don't you tell me that I've been imagining your reactions to me? I am beyond the point of telling myself that it's all a figment of my imagination. God help me, this is the last thing I expected, but then how true the motto that the unexpected is always lying just around the corner…' His mouth traced the curve of her jawbone. 'Tell me you don't want this and I'll leave you in peace for ever. No tabs kept over my brother. If you decide to walk up the aisle with him, no matter your reasons would be misguided, you won't find me interfering.'

'I'm not the kind of girl who…sleeps around…'

Theo was quick to pick up on the incongruity of her statement. 'But you're the kind of girl who would marry a man she isn't attracted to physically simply for the sake of security. A far more dubious morality, some might think.'

Abby twisted away from him. There was no answer to his bald statement. 'It isn't all about sex.'

'I'm going to take you upstairs. This is no place to make love and, don't worry, I will be very gentle with you.'

Abby was melting. With every step up those stairs, which he mounted as silently and as quickly as a cat, she could feel her body roaring in wild response, wanting him in a way she had never thought she could ever want a man again, wanting him more than she could remember ever wanting Oliver, but then that would be, she guessed, because she had been untouched for years.

He pushed open her door with his shoulder, locking it behind him, and then lay her on the bed. Her silence was as telling as a flurry of words. Her brain was telling her to stop but her body didn't want to listen. Theo turned on the small lamp by the chest of drawers, which was just bright enough to show the silhouettes of their figures, and wondered what he would do if she turned him away now. His body was screaming for satisfaction, but he would walk away, admittedly to have a very cold shower, and once he had started walking he wouldn't stop. But, God, that thought rocked him more than he cared to admit.

'Your time for outrage and protests is fast coming to an end,' he said roughly, pausing at the foot of the bed and devouring her hungrily with his eyes. The soft folds of her very sensible knee-length skirt had ridden up to expose the slim paleness of her thighs and her eyes were very wide. To be stared at like that, unwilling but compelled, made his groins ache with desire. He slowly began to unbutton his shirt, looking at her looking at him. He removed it and tossed it on the ground without taking his eyes off her face, only pausing as his fingers rested at the waistband of his trousers. Beyond this point there would be no going back but, God, it was difficult, when every instinct made him want to rip his clothes off and take her, caveman style. Forget about the art of seduction and finesse. He just wanted to be in her and to feel her enclose him.

'Don't stop,' Abby whispered. Her words dropped into the thick silence with the finality of a door closing, and she didn't care. Didn't care if sex was the only dish on the menu, didn't care if he thought her a woman of dubious principles, didn't care about anything but having this big man possess her utterly and completely.

He had said that he would be gentle with her and she knew he had to be, although her foot felt fine, but she was shocked to discover that she didn't want gentle, she wanted hot and rough.

She watched as he continued to remove his clothes and groaned softly when the last item of clothing finally joined the gathering bundle on the floor. The man was magnificent. Broad shoulders, hard, well-toned torso, tapering to a manhood that left her in no doubt that he was as turned on by her as she was by him. When he lightly touched himself she couldn't help a full-throated groan escaping her lips. She felt more than damp. One touch and she would explode.

'Like what you see, Abby?' he asked thickly and she nodded.

'Your turn now.' He gave her a slow smile and she smiled back shyly.

'You might not care for what you see, Theo. I'm not one of your voluptuous types.'

'I've already had a sneak preview, in case you'd forgotten, and believe me I liked what I saw. And no, don't take anything off. I want to savour that myself.'

Conscious of her foot, Theo moved over her until he was straddling her, then he helped her off with the T-shirt. When she would have unclasped the bra from behind, he stopped her.

'Bit by bit,' he whispered. Lord, his hands were shaking, like a teenager having his first sexual encounter! Amazing. The consummate lover had suddenly turned into a rash, green youth barely able to contain himself! He had thought about those breasts so often, but as he pulled down the straps of her bra he was flooded with a powerful surge of lust. Those sexy big nipples with their stiffened peaks were the pinnacle of beauty. He would taste them soon enough, enjoy the pleasure of licking them and the heady thrill of feeling her squirm under his exploring tongue. But for now there was more to see, so much more. He removed her bra, freeing those wonderful breasts fully to his gaze and for a few moments was content to just devour them with his eyes, noting the way her chest rose and fell with her hot, quick breathing.

Then, slowly and carefully, he pulled down the elasticated skirt. Her body was slender and firm with a boyish grace to it that made him wonder how he could ever have found those full-chested curvaceous bodies a turn-on. He hooked his fingers into the sides of her briefs and very slowly drew those down and breathed in sharply as her nakedness was finally exposed. Fair, soft hair covering the place he needed so badly to taste. It took mammoth will-power to remember that he had to be very gentle. And gentle he was, as he leaned down over her to kiss her parted mouth, thrusting his tongue against hers but taking his time, working his way downwards from mouth to neck, from neck to breasts, where he lost himself in the delight of suckling on them. Then lower still, to trail his tongue against the flat planes of her stomach, to circle the delicate indent of her navel, then down to the honeyed moistness between her legs. He placed his hands on the sides of her thighs and, with a muted groan, inserted his questing tongue into that slit, seeking and finding the little bud and teasing it until she could no longer contain her soft moans, little whimpers urging him on as her hand pressed against the back of his head and her legs widened to accommodate his hungry mouth…

CHAPTER NINE

ABBY watched lazily from the bed as Theo got dressed. She loved this and hated it. Loved it because she just loved watching him and hated it because it marked the end of the weekend, and the end of every weekend brought her closer to losing him.

She still found it hard to believe that she was in the position she now found herself, in thrall to a lover who didn't love her, addicted to his personality with a compulsion that wasn't reciprocated and terrified of the inevitable loss. Not once in the past six weeks had he murmured any meaningful endearment to her. Not even in the throes of passion, and surely there was no passion beyond what they had shared?

He enjoyed her and he told her so, but love...? No. He might not see her as the classic gold-digger, but at the back of his mind she was still the woman who had been happy to sell her own personal principles for the sake of financial and emotional security. She had used his brother, whether she wanted to admit it or not, and so he had no qualms about using her.

It was the worst of all possible situations but she still accepted it because she just couldn't help herself.

He travelled to see her on the Friday, sometimes on Saturday, and he always, always left on the Sunday night, after Jamie had been settled in bed. Whether he was in Athens, or more frequently than not in London, he made the journey.

But it was all about the sex. At least for him. She

wasn't even sure that he liked himself for the weakness. There were times at the height of their lovemaking when he would refer to her as his little witch and she was sadly aware that the words were not spoken as a compliment.

But here she was, loving him more with each passing weekend, and knowing that she was a fool. He might not have been married like Oliver but he was as dangerous to her health. More. Because what she had felt for Oliver had been an insignificant infatuation compared to what she felt for the man lazily slipping on his trousers with his back to her.

'I can feel you thinking,' he drawled, not turning round to look at her, busying himself with putting on his shirt, which he didn't bother to tuck into his waistband. 'What are you thinking about?'

About us and where we're going, she wanted to answer. *About what will happen to me when you get bored with me and decide to move on. Will you even let me know or will you just fail to turn up one evening when I'm expecting you? After all, a woman with no moral ethics doesn't deserve the dignity of a farewell, does she?*

'Oh nothing. Work tomorrow, I guess. I hate Mondays.'

'You could always quit.' Theo turned to face her and continued buttoning up his shirt before leaning against the squat wrought iron rail at the foot of her bed.

'Oh, yes. What a good idea. I can quit and spend my time waiting for the money to start growing on the trees in the back garden.' She laughed to find that he wasn't laughing back. 'You're kidding, aren't you?' She felt his eyes roving over her naked body. He liked looking at her when he dressed and she had discovered that she liked it too, liked that wanton feeling she got when he was fully clothed and she had not a strip on.

'I'm a rich man.' He shrugged casually but his eyes were sharp and watchful. 'I can afford to support you.'

Abby struggled not to react to his words as though they were a slap in her face.

'You mean you can afford to buy me.'

'I don't need to buy you, Abby. You are already mine for the taking.'

'God, Theo.' She rolled over on to her side and yanked the duvet cover over her. 'Sometimes you amaze me.' Tears pricked the back of her eyelids and she bit down on them.

'I'm merely stating a fact.' He moved around the bed and sat next to her, swinging her round to face him when she would have turned away. 'You're exhausted by the end of the week. What's so wrong in a man wanting to do something about his mistress's exhaustion? It makes perfect sense to me.'

'Which just shows what different planets we live on, because it makes no sense to me whatsoever. I like my independence, I like earning my own money and not being reliant on anyone.'

'You were prepared to be reliant on my brother,' Theo pointed out. Bad idea, he thought, bringing Michael into the conversation when he was about to leave. He knew that she still saw him occasionally during the week, that he would sometimes take her and Jamie out for a meal somewhere, or else just treat them to a seat in one of his restaurants so that he could sit with them and chat even for a few minutes at a time. All's fair in love and war, Theo had thought. Michael had lost her, however much they made of their friendship, but the thought still nagged away at him like a slow-burning fire that was always too close to shooting up sparks for his comfort.

Abby looked at him and remained stoutly silent. She

and Michael had kept their secret but she knew that their
continued relationship got on Theo's nerves. He wasn't
jealous; no, that wasn't it. She was his disposable object
of desire. What he didn't like was that the situation between her and Michael should have ended in something
final. The fact that it hadn't made it messy as far as Theo
was concerned.

'Well?' Theo pressed home, ignoring the voice in his
head telling him to leave it alone. 'If anything, I am in
a far stronger financial position to take care of your
needs, so where's the problem?' He could feel the slow-
burning fire begin to gather momentum. 'I also think that
Jamie should go to a private school. He's too bright for
any old school.'

Abby was momentarily distracted by the mention of
her son. Theo rarely discussed him, but he was brilliant
with Jamie. He seemed to have just the right knack of
knowing how to communicate with him, man to boy, and
Jamie adored it.

Another complication she would have to address some
time soon.

She had originally started off with all the right intentions. She had yielded to their overpowering attraction
for one another and had told herself that there was nothing wrong in clutching at some passing happiness and
enjoying the freedom of a purely sexual relationship. She
had tried to keep Jamie out of the picture but it had been
hard. Now, during the day, they did things as a threesome
and it was so enjoyable watching her son light up like a
Christmas tree whenever Theo was around that she had
lowered her defences and gone along for the ride.

Somewhere along the line, things had begun to go
badly wrong and she had not made a move to stop
any of it.

'My son's education is none of your business, Theo.'

Theo felt his body tense and then immediately told himself that she was absolutely right and thank God for that. 'I'm merely putting forward a point of view.'

'Thank you. But really, I can't possibly afford to think of sending Jamie to a private school.'

'*You* don't have to afford anything,' he said impatiently. '*I* can afford it.'

'Can we talk about this another time?'

'In a couple of months' time, you mean? We've almost had that. Shall we wait for another two?'

Abby sat up and looked at him, mouth open, as a sudden thought began to gather pace, galloping with clattering, panicky hooves through her brain.

'What did you say?' she asked, dry-mouthed, and Theo looked back at her through narrowed eyes.

'What's the matter?'

'Sorry? What?' Abby blinked at him, desperate for him to leave so that she could consult the diary in her handbag.

'Forget it. I've got to go now.' He swooped round so that he was sitting on the bed by her. Frequently, his departures were delayed because one touch and they couldn't seem to stop themselves from climbing right back into bed. This time, Abby was barely aware of him tilting her chin up so that he could look at her squarely in the face, hardly noticed the brief touch of his mouth against hers.

'Amazing. I still can't seem to get enough of you,' he murmured. He trailed his fingers through her hair and watched, fascinated as always, by the startling contrast between that spectacular blondeness against the tan of his own skin.

'Yes, that's quite something, isn't it, Theo?' Abby returned more sharply than she had intended.

'Meaning?' he enquired with sudden coolness in his voice.

'Meaning that most normal human beings wouldn't really see a couple of months as an amazing feat of endurance.' She smiled wanly to dispel the little burst of sarcasm. She had learnt early on not to trip up on any relationship issues. 'But then,' she teased, 'we both know that you're not a normal human being.'

'Hopefully that doesn't stop me functioning in all the right places,' he murmured in that husky, sexy voice of his that could turn her to jelly.

'You should go. It's already after eleven. Lord knows how you manage to function on so little sleep.' She stroked the side of his face, loving the feel of his skin against her palm.

'You forget. I'm not a normal human being. I don't need the normal amount of sleep.'

'Which isn't to say that you shouldn't try. Even the toughest of men can get tired and that's when illnesses start kicking in.'

'Nice to know you care, sweetheart.' He laughed and subjected her to a lingering kiss that was followed by a lazy exploration of her breasts. *Something sweet to take away with me on the trip back*, he told himself, looking up from the nipple on which he had been lavishing his attention. The diary waiting in her handbag momentarily faded into insignificance as she lay back with a sigh to enjoy the feel of his mouth curving around her nipple, licking and sucking, a man enjoying a feast. Her fingers were curled in his hair, which he had grown a bit longer now at her insistence.

'It seems that I'm a bit hungrier than I thought...' he murmured, giving her a wicked grin.

'Theo, you should really go...' Was that her voice? Weak with helpless desire? 'Besides, I have an early start tomorrow...'

'So I won't be long...' He pulled aside the duvet which she had dragged over herself earlier, when some spark of common sense had still been functioning, and parted her legs so that he could bury his mouth against her soft, moist femininity, drawing out a muted gasp of pleasure as he tasted the honeyed core of her.

Satisfying himself took a back seat to satisfying her, and this he did with a thoroughness that had her squirming under him, arching up to meet his questing tongue, tightening her hands into fists that clutched the duvet. He could feel that little bud tightening and blossoming under his tongue and he felt her burst of uncontrollable pleasure as she reached the peak of her excitement and her body took over, convulsing as wave after wave of sexual fulfilment rocked her.

Abby looked at him drowsily when he finally moved up to plant a feathery kiss against the corner of her mouth.

'Sweet dreams,' he said. 'Just so long as they are of me and only me.'

'As if I would dare dream of anyone else,' she whispered truthfully. *As if I could.*

She was very tempted simply to fall asleep when she heard the click of the front door closing behind him, but the temptation lasted only long enough for her to realise that falling asleep on a potential problem didn't actually go a long way to solving it.

Not, she feverishly told herself as she tiptoed downstairs, clutching her dressing gown around her, that there was going to be a problem. Not, she thought, as she realised that her period was late, that that meant anything. Her body clock had never behaved in a predictable fashion and, besides, she was on the Pill so she couldn't possibly be pregnant.

When she had been pregnant with Jamie she had had all sorts of symptoms. She was a symptom-free zone, which meant that there was nothing to worry about.

She virtually didn't need to go through the trouble of buying a kit to prove what she knew it was destined to prove, but she spent the following morning barely able to concentrate and by twelve-thirty her feet had somehow managed to take her to the chemist on what she told herself over and over was a wasted trip.

It had to be.

It required a will of steel not to sneak to the bathroom during the course of what was a very busy afternoon to put her nerves to rest.

Later, much later, she wondered whether she hadn't already known, deep down, that she would receive the information she didn't want, that she couldn't possibly behave in a normal manner at work if she did. Hence her decision to wait until Jamie had finally gone to bed at a little after seven.

In the darkness of her bedroom she lay on the bed and tried to get her mind around the nightmare that she was indeed pregnant. She couldn't work out how, except to assume that the Pill, that small white tablet, had failed at the worst possible moment. She had had a tummy upset, she remembered. Had it been then? Did it matter anyway?

Every muscle and nerve in her body was rigid with tension as she tried to find a way forward through the mess. She couldn't tell Theo. She attempted to picture the conversation, struggled to think how she could just drop that little nugget of a bombshell into their conversation. How would he react?

Just thinking about it made her feel sick.

Here was a man who didn't want a relationship and especially would never consider a relationship with her. He would be coldly, unspeakably furious. He might even think that she had done it deliberately to trap him into a situation he would never have offered of his own free will. Worse, he would probably insist on taking over financial responsibility. Another horrifying thought struck her. Would he want more than financial responsibility? Would he want to take the baby away from her, bring it up in some traditional Greek way?

Tears gathered in the corners of her eyes and she didn't bother wiping them away as they trickled down the side of her face.

She wanted to imagine a sane conclusion to any conversation she might have with Theo about his sudden, unwanted escalation to fatherhood, but couldn't. It was just beyond the realms of her imagination. Theo might have shown her another side of him over the past few weeks, but the side that had attacked her when they had first met was still there. It hadn't been some lunatic aberration.

She fell asleep when her brain could no longer deal with the enormity of her nightmare and woke up with only a few seconds of blissful peace before the nightmare resumed its relentless pacing.

This was so much worse than when she had discovered that she was pregnant with Jamie. At least then she had wallowed in the optimism that Oliver would be happy, that they would be together, one sweet little family unit. When her hopes had been dashed there was no speculation about what would happen next in the scenario. She would raise her baby by herself and Oliver would disappear.

This time round, there was no optimism. There was likewise no certainty as to where the road would take her, and the more she laboured the unhappy options the more she realised that Theo wasn't simply going to walk away and wash his hands of his child. Whether he liked to admit it or not, he was a natural father. She had seen that in the way he dealt with her own son.

No, Theo would either remove his baby from her custody, which wouldn't be difficult—he was a man of enormous wealth and influence and she was a single mother struggling to make ends meet—or else he would insist on sharing custody, which would entail years of contact with him, years of watching the man she loved turn into a stranger who hated her, who only communicated with her through lack of choice. He would find his own love and she would always be there, forced to stand on the sidelines and watch while her own life shrivelled up and disappeared.

It was only when the end of the week drew closer that she began to see a tentative light at the end of the dark tunnel.

Not a very morally uplifting light, she had to admit, but a light nevertheless.

He had asked whether she would accept his financial handouts, become his paid mistress in effect. Naturally, she had thrown his offer back in his face, but she would re-introduce the subject, make sure that she stepped over the lines she had been scrupulously avoiding for weeks. She would ask him about their relationship. Just one scrap of hope and she would tell him, she would trust in the blind hope that they could reach an amicable solution.

Surely, if there was some affection, it wouldn't be a complete impossibility? She could work from amicable.

If there was nothing, then she would break off the relationship and disappear. It would mean leaving behind dear, dear Michael, but how else could she play it?

She was still a bag of nerves when Friday rolled round, however. He had called to tell her what time to expect him, and as usual he had told her how much he had missed her, missed her sexy body, missed waking up next to her in bed. Abby tried to sound natural and wondered how long those sentiments would last if he were to find out that the sexy body was *en route* to becoming a fairly sizeable one.

He was, he said, going to be with her by ten. Meetings had overrun during the day, he said regretfully, hence the ridiculous hour.

'I'm kind of tired anyway,' Abby said down the end of the line and she was aware of silence as the seconds ticked by. She was pulling back and he was too sharp to miss it, but what else could she do? Her head hurt from thinking and all her thoughts led in one direction. No more Theo. No more blissful, wonderful, earth-shattering sex and the blossoming of being in the company of the man she loved. 'It's been a long week,' she said shortly, thinking that no truer word had been spoken. 'There was a problem with the computer system and everything seemed to take ten times longer than it should. No one's fault, but it did mean that we all ended up working overtime just to keep on top of things.'

'We'll discuss this when we meet,' Theo said shortly.

For the first time since their fragile affair had begun, she was treated to the soft click of disconnection. An ominous warning of things to come, she decided.

Even more ominously, he was late, though full of apologies when he finally walked through the door at a little after eleven.

'Apologies and champagne,' he said with a grin, spinning her round to face him when she was ready to head for the kitchen. Too much looking at him and her sense of purpose would evaporate like a puff of smoke. Now that she had braced herself for walking away she realised, belatedly, just how much he had got under her skin. It wasn't sufficient that she knew every inch of his face, the way his eyes followed her in that lazy, sexy way of his, the way his mouth curved into a smile that held the promise of untold excitement. She even, she realised bleakly, knew his smell. It was clean, with just a hint of aftershave, and very, very masculine.

'What's the matter?' Theo asked sharply, tangling his fingers in her hair so that she was obliged to remain where she was and meet his penetrating gaze.

'Nothing.'

'Nothing? Is that why, for the first time, you're suddenly *tired*?'

'People get tired, Theo. Not everyone has your stamina.' She dropped her eyes, hoping to maintain some semblance of control, although she could feel her heart thudding out of control. 'And thanks for the champagne. Honestly. But I think I'd fall asleep over the first glass.'

'I told you my solution to your exhaustion problem.' He dumped the bottle on the sideboard by the door, shrugged off his jacket, and then before she could protest scooped her off her feet and headed for the sitting room. 'Normally,' he murmured, 'I wouldn't be heading in this direction, but we need to talk. Lifting you like this reminds me of that first night, when you sprained your ankle. Remember? I held you and you filled my nostrils.

Did I ever tell you that at that very moment I knew that I wanted you?'

The word *want* was like a shard of glass cutting into her heart. She shook her head dumbly and allowed herself to be placed on to the sofa, feet on his lap so that he could massage them.

'You're right. We need to talk, Theo.'

His hand stilled for a few seconds before he continued the languorous caress of her feet.

'You've thought about my offer to you?' he prompted, and Abby could hear the thread of satisfaction in his voice. Of course, it wouldn't have crossed his mind that she might seriously turn him down. She drew her feet up, tucking them under her, well out of reach of his seductive fingers.

'I thought about it and...' she wondered how to phrase what she needed to say '...I don't know why you would want to support me. I thought you despised the kind of woman who looks to a man for her upkeep.'

'I never said I *despised* that kind of woman,' Theo said irritably. 'I said I despised women who set out to trap men into supporting them.'

'How can you think of paying for me? How long would it last? You must know that...well...'

'Go on.'

His voice was not encouraging and Abby swallowed painfully. 'We've been seeing each other now for nearly two months,' she began falteringly. 'I'd like to know where you see this relationship going. I mean, in the long term, so to speak.'

'*In the long term?*' Theo looked at her narrowly. 'Is that what this mood of yours is about? You're concerned that I might be on the verge of dumping you?'

'You're prone to boredom when it comes to women. You've told me that yourself.'

'You don't bore me.'

'Not yet, anyway.' They stared at one another. Theo, she noticed, looked as though he had taken a sip of his coffee only to find that the milk was off. If the situation wasn't so serious it would almost be comical.

'What do you want me to say, Abby?'

'I want you to tell me where you think we're going. It's not the most difficult question in the world to answer.'

'How do I know where we're going? I don't possess a crystal ball!'

'But face it, I'm not the sort of woman you ever had in mind for any kind of long-term relationship, am I?' she asked. The time for beating about the bush was over and done with. Now, all the questions she had diplomatically shelved were coming out of their hiding places. 'I'm a woman who was involved with your brother.' She ticked that off on one finger. 'I'm English. I have a child by someone else. I could never represent a union of dynasties, like that…like that girl you were introduced to at your grandfather's party in Santorini!'

'No. You're right. You're not the sort of woman I ever contemplated being married to.'

The finality of his words dropped into the silence between them like poison. So, what had she expected? That he would warmly talk to her about commitment? Maybe throw love into the conversation?

Theo watched the defeat settle over her features like a shadow. Really, he didn't know why he hadn't anticipated this. He should have known sooner or later that she would want more out of a relationship than the simple pleasure of enjoying each other's bodies. Best this way, he thought. Ever since he had met her, he had stopped focusing on the only thing in life worth focusing on, namely his work. She was in his head far too much and he hadn't been lying when he had told her that she was not the sort of woman he would ever marry. His eventual marriage had more or less been planned in his head. Marriage to a Greek woman, probably with the same vast connections that he had. Yes, call it a meeting of dynasties, he thought irritably to himself. It sounded cold but it would be practical, and practical things lasted. He looked at her soft face, now unreadable, and was angry with himself for the sharp jab of confusion and panic he felt at the thought of no longer seeing her, touching her, being with her.

'How do you imagine that I could ever consider a long-term relationship with you when at the back of my mind I'm all too aware that you were prepared to offer yourself to my brother for the wrong reasons? I'm not a monster but I am, I like to think, fairly intelligent.' Theo's voice was coldly detached.

Abby didn't say anything. She looked away, eyes glazed with tears, and chewed on her fingernail.

'What's to say that you have not switched allegiances to me because I am a better financial bet than my brother and one you fancy into the bargain?'

'That's cruel and unfair!'

'That's called the ruthless march of logic.'

'And there's no room in your life for anything but the ruthless march of logic, is there? Even relationships and commitment have to be logical, don't they, Theo? A logical, committed relationship requires the right girl with the right credentials, and, well, there's no room in your life for the illogical, is there? No, that would be a crime in the world of Theo Toyas!'

'This is a ridiculous conversation.'

'This is a *necessary* conversation. Any girl, even one with all the wrong credentials, eventually wants to know where she's going.'

'And where did you think we'd end up, Abby? Walking down the aisle? I thought we both enjoyed where we were.' He sighed heavily. 'Why spoil things?'

'I think it's time you left now.'

'This is crazy!' He stood up and began pacing the room. He slammed his fist on the wall and was grimly satisfied when she swung around to look at him. That remarkable hair, which he had brushed, played with, threaded through his fingers, hung around her like a fall of vanilla silk. His hands itched to touch it again, to touch *her* again, and his weakness was driving him crazy. He paused to position himself right by her, then leaned over her, face darkly angry.

'Why ask questions about a future when you can destroy the present in the process?'

Abby thought of the life growing inside her. Actually, she wanted to say, I have a pretty good reason now that you mention it. She didn't need much of an imagination to figure out what his reaction would be.

'You don't even sound as though you *like* me, Theo,' she said hollowly.

'For God's sake! Of course I *like* you!' He pushed himself away from her. 'What sort of self-pitying remark is that?'

Abby didn't look at him. She stared straight ahead at the door of the sitting room, which was almost closed. She needed him to go. Soon. Now. Just having him share her space was tearing her to shreds.

'Well?' he demanded harshly. 'Do you think I would ever sleep with a woman I didn't *like*?'

Abby shrugged. 'You tell me, Theo. Would you? It's not so very much worse than sleeping with a woman you don't *trust*, is it?'

When he didn't immediately answer she inclined her head to look at him. He was leaning against the wall, hands thrust aggressively into his pockets. She knew that as far as he was concerned trust didn't enter into the equation. Just so long as she didn't demand anything of him, didn't try to pin him down, then things were fine. He could dispense money, could talk about maintaining her, but as long as the situation remained fully within his control he could continue to enjoy what they had. Asking for more raised ugly questions.

'You're determined to push this to a conclusion, aren't you?' He interpreted her silence for assent. 'How could you ever expect that I would trust you?'

'Because...'

'Because we made a good team between the sheets?'

That stung. Control was now something very small bobbing about on rough seas, something she was finding difficult to get a hold of.

Was that all he saw? The laughter, the times they had shared with Jamie, the conversation...did it all come down, for him, to a necessary part of getting her between those sheets so that he could have a good time? She couldn't believe it, but that was what he was saying, wasn't it? She bit back the dam waiting to burst and gathered herself together sufficiently to point to the sitting room door. No shaking finger. That would come later.

'Out.'

'When I walk through that door I won't be walking back,' Theo said grimly. 'I have never begged for a woman and I am certainly not intending to start now.'

Abby, who couldn't bear to look at him, gritted her teeth. Prolonging the conversation was a waste of time. She could never convince him that he could trust her and, even if she could, it would make no difference. He didn't love her and he never would.

She was aware of him moving but it was only when he came into her line of vision, when he had pulled open the door and was standing there, starkly silhouetted by the light in the hall shining behind him, that she truly looked at him.

'What will you tell Jamie?' Theo asked roughly.

'Do you care?' She saw his jaw clench and his face darkened. 'I'll tell him that…that you had to return to Greece and that we probably won't be seeing you again… He'll understand. Kids adapt. He'll have forgotten all about you in two weeks' time.' She barely noticed the shadow that crossed his face at those words. Her mind was already vaulting ahead to a life without him in it.

'Right.' Dammit! She wouldn't even look at him! He had walked through that front door with champagne and apologies. He was leaving with a sackful of memories. And, he told himself, it was for the best. She had been a pleasing distraction but that was it and it would have been unfair on her to have continued what they had for longer anyway. But she still wasn't looking at him. He felt stupidly deprived of his right to leave on the last word.

In the end he simply turned his back, gathering his jacket *en route*, leaving with a quiet click of the front door.

Released from the tension, Abby felt herself go limp like a rag doll. She almost expected to hear the ring of the doorbell, could hardly believe that everything could end so quickly and quietly, but there was no ring and, after a couple of moments, she heard the sound of his engine starting and the crunch of the tyres as he sped away from her and her life.

Then, and only then, did the tears come.

Later, when the tears had dried up, still sitting on the sofa in the sitting room because her body couldn't contemplate the exertion of mounting the stairs to the bedroom, she considered what she would have to do next.

Leave Brighton. Her stomach was flat now but it wouldn't be in a couple of months' time and there was no way she could risk being seen by him accidentally should he come down to visit his brother. Leave Brighton like a thief in the night and face pregnancy on her own. Again.

Her parents might have roamed all four corners of England and finally ended up on the other side of the world, but they had stayed together in a loving, united relationship. Whereas she…

She rested her hand on her stomach and closed her eyes. Well, there was no point feeling sorry for herself. She had to carry on and she would do it the best she could.

CHAPTER TEN

'YOU'RE moping again, Abby. You really can't afford to, you know. Jamie senses it and it makes him unhappy.'

Abby looked at her mother and dredged a smile up from somewhere. Since when had her mother ever been *brisk*? Then again, since when had her mother ever worn her hair in a neat, short, tailored style and dressed in a *trouser suit*?

The past four weeks had been a series of revelations and frenetic action, and all because she had picked the phone up the day after Theo had walked out through her front door for ever and called her parents.

She had expected vague sympathies and some sort of faraway offer to bring her over to Australia just as soon as they got their act together and started saving some money. That had always been their refrain.

Instead, she had got some crisp no-nonsense advice from her mother and an immediate decision to fly to England so that she could take her daughter in hand.

That had been three and a half weeks ago and during that time she had sold her small house in Brighton, accompanied her mother on an energy-fuelled property hunting foray in Cornwall and received all the down-to-earth, sensible words of comfort she had never in a million years expected.

Right now they were looking around a cottage, the fifth property they had seen in as many days.

'Right. What do you think?' Mary Clinton pulled out her stenographer's pad, in which she had been making comprehensive notes about every house they had looked around, and began jotting a few things down.

'Mum…I don't know…what if it doesn't work? What if you hate it here? I mean, you've lived with dad in Melbourne for such a long time and Cornwall…well, Cornwall isn't Melbourne…'

'I gathered that straight away.' Her mother quietly shut the pad and looked at her daughter's drained, pretty face. 'But the time is right to move. We were going to make the move early next year, surprise you with a Christmas visit to break the news, but now is as good a time as any. Better. Moving in the depths of winter wouldn't have been much fun, would it? As it stands, we can all celebrate Christmas together in a new house in a new place…' She patted her short fair hair thoughtfully. Really, Abby mused, her mother looked like a million dollars. Her face glowed with good health and she had lost none of the willowy slenderness she had had as a young woman. It was just encased in vastly different clothing. No more long, flowing skirts and cheesecloth tops. Instead, smart grey trousers, neat brogues and a snappy little jacket that hugged her figure.

But then, as she had discovered over the many conversations they had shared over the weeks, times had changed for her parents. Their organic food shop had gradually turned into a first class restaurant and the ethnic ornaments had become such successful sellers that they had opened a shop. They had, in effect, become entrepreneurs in their middle age. Her father had brushed up on his business skills and handled all the books. Her mother had become an astute buyer. Together, their vague venture had turned slowly but surely into a hugely profitable concern, and the move to Cornwall was really a business expansion. A friend and manager would continue to run their concern in Melbourne, the eventual plan being to convert the profits into a small, specialised hotel, catering for tourists who wanted unusual surroundings and purely organic food.

According to her mother, the market in Cornwall was ripe for a similar enterprise. There was a great deal of money flying around, there were tourists and there was a substantial number of people willing to pay for something just a little bit different when it came to accommodation and cuisine.

They had discussed the business venture over cups of tea and glasses of wine, they had talked about Abby moving in with them, helping them run their business for as long as she wanted. The only thing they never seemed to talk about was Theo, and Abby knew that that was her fault. Her mother would have been happy to talk about what had happened but somehow Abby just couldn't bring herself to dwell on it. Maybe in time. It still hurt too much to think about him. So she had dispensed the barest bones of information and repeatedly changed the subject until her mother had got the message. In time, she would open up but not yet.

The only thing that stopped her succumbing to despair was Jamie. He had embraced his newly found grandmother with childish, unquestioning enthusiasm and had greeted news of a move to Cornwall without trepidation. He was a ray of light in her twilit world.

She had also not disappeared completely from Michael's life. They would continue to communicate, though chances were that she would seldom see him, but he would always be a link and at the moment that helped. Just knowing that he knew how she felt about his brother, knowing that he would feed her titbits of information if ever she asked, although she had warned him never to mention Theo unless she brought the subject up. In due course, she might even tell him about the pregnancy although she wasn't sure that it would ever be fair to put him in such an untenable position.

She surfaced from her thoughts to realise that her mother was speculating on putting an offer on the cottage, was planning what might go where and how the bedrooms would work, with Abby and Jamie having the rooms at the back, overlooking the distant view of the sea.

Which seemed to remind Jamie that he had been promised a trip to the beach for a little walk.

'You needn't come, love,' Mary said, catching her daughter's mood and knowing that the best thing she could do would be to take Jamie out for an hour or so. She hated to see her daughter wrapped up in unhappy thoughts, but the grieving process had to be endured to be overcome. In time, this man who had hurt her would become a part of her past and she would move on. In the meanwhile, she would simply have to face her misery and learn to accommodate it into her life.

Abby smiled gratefully at her mother and remained sitting at the kitchen table, watching as Jamie slid his small hand into her mother's. They disappeared from view and she continued to sit, looking out of the window, not really focusing on anything at all. After ten minutes of sitting, she listlessly did a tour of the cottage herself so that she could try and work up some spark of enthusiasm. Oh, she was happy to be away from Brighton and out of that house that held too many memories but, even with such a dramatic change of scenery to help her, she still felt flat and tired. The fact that she was two months' pregnant didn't help her energy levels, although increasingly it did give her a sense of quiet contentment that there would always be a part of Theo with her when this baby was born.

She heard the crunch of tyres on gravel as she was descending the staircase and assumed it would be the estate agent. They were nothing if not aggressive in their follow-up techniques.

Just a shame that they had missed her mother by a quarter of an hour, because Mary Clinton knew how to deal with them. Lord knew when she had developed that thread of steel, but Abby had been very grateful for it on more than one occasion when she just couldn't be bothered to tackle the day-to-day realities that had needed tackling.

The polite knock on the door had turned into a more insistent rapping and she wondered, fleetingly, whether there was any hope of hiding. Considering the man would have a key, she abandoned the idea because being caught under the kitchen table would not be dignified. She pulled open the door and blinked. The sun was bright and sharp and threw the man's silhouette into dark perspective. Abby shaded her eyes with one hand and then a whirling dizziness began to spread through her, radiating out from deep inside until it was filling every inch of her body. She was barely aware of breathing and had only a second's warning that she was going to faint.

She came to to find herself lying flat on a sofa in the living room. For a few disorienting moments she wondered whether she had dozed off and had had some wildly improbable nightmare, then her eyes fluttered open and there he was, kneeling on the floor beside her. Abby closed her eyes quickly and re-opened them, knowing that the spectre next to her would disappear. It didn't. It spoke.

'You fainted. If you wait a few seconds I'll get you some water.'

'What are you doing here?' Abby asked weakly. She pulled herself into a sitting position and gaped at the man calmly staring back down at her.

The weeks since she had seen him had etched lines of strain into his face. The dark eyes were shuttered.

'I went to your house. Imagine my surprise when I discovered that it had been sold. All in the space of two weeks!'

'Why?' She shuffled up a little higher and carried on looking at him as though she had seen a ghost. 'Why have you come here? How did you find me?' With every syllable her panicked voice rose one notch higher.

'Which question do you want me to answer first? I'll start with the easier one, shall I?' He moved away, which was a relief, but only to drag a chair across to the sofa so that he could reposition himself a bit more comfortably. 'I went to see my brother. He had been trying to get through to me urgently, but I wasn't taking calls. In the end, I decided to drive to Brighton and talk with him face to face. Why didn't you tell me?'

'Tell you what?'

'Why did you let me think...' He tore his eyes away from her and sat back, folding his arms. His expression was fiercely, intensely vulnerable. Abby, too shocked by his arrival, just watched and waited. When he next spoke, his voice was controlled and even but it was costing him effort. 'I've been to hell and back these past four weeks...'

'Sorry?' Abby whispered.

'I wasn't expecting to find you here on your own. I thought your mother and Jamie might have been with you. I was hoping for…' haggard eyes swept over her face '…a little time before I launched into this speech…'

'You *prepared a speech*?'

'Michael told me that your mother had come over, that you were thinking of moving to Cornwall. A pretty big place to start looking for a slip of a girl, and I'm not sure it wouldn't have taken a hell of a lot longer if I hadn't found your postcard on his mantelpiece. *Missing Brighton but glad to be out. Will call soon,* the card said. I telephoned every estate agent in the book until I came across the one you had used to see this place.' He laughed wryly. 'I never thought I had the makings of a detective, but it would seem that strange situations reveal hidden talents.'

'I still don't understand…'

'Nor do I.' For the first time, he met her eyes directly and smiled with faint bemusement. 'I've spent the past four weeks waiting for my life to return to normal, waiting to be interested and focused in my work, waiting for my food to taste like food and for my social companions to amuse me. It didn't happen. The only person I could think about was…was you.'

Abby's mouth dropped open and she discovered that she could hardly breathe. A sweet buzzing filled her ears. *If this is a dream,* she thought, *then let me sleep for ever.*

'Michael called repeatedly and I refused to take any of his calls. Just thinking about him, thinking that I might never see you again but he would, filled me with rage. And, yes, jealousy.'

She saw the dark flush spread over his face and her heart soared. It would have taken enormous honesty to have admitted to that and she loved him for it.

'In the end, though, I had to see him. And he told me everything and I just want to know…'

'What did he tell you?' Abby whispered.

'He told me about his sexuality, that he is gay, that your engagement was something you both cooked up between yourselves. He said that it gave him respectability with the family and it gave you safety from undesirable men.'

'Poor Michael.' Her eyes filled up. 'That must have been the hardest thing he ever had to do. He was so afraid of disappointing you and your mother.' She wiped her eyes with the back of her hand. 'I couldn't breathe a word, Theo.'

'Instead you let me believe…'

'I had no choice.'

'And I love you for that.'

For a few precious moments time stood still as she savoured the words she had longed to hear. *He loved her!* This big, powerful, controlled, invincible man loved her! The thought of his baby inside her, the secret she had kept from him, brought her down to earth with a painful bump. She swallowed hard and stood up, turning her back to him and walking towards the window, arms folded, body language expressive.

Theo watched and felt a chill of pure fear snake through him. This, he thought, isn't right. He hadn't had a plan when he had driven like a lunatic down to Cornwall, covering the distance in record time, clutching the names of the two cottages they were due to see. He had just known that he had to see her, had to express what he had kept hidden from himself until he couldn't hide it any longer. His love had been an uncontainable force.

God, what had he thought? Certainly not that he would open his heart and still have to endure watching her walk away from him, because that was what she was doing now. He could feel it in his bones. The way she was standing, clasping herself protectively, the distance she had put between them, the closed, uncertain expression on her face. None of this had been part of his plan.

'Theo…'

'Don't say it,' Theo answered harshly. 'I said too much.' He stood up and shoved his hands into his pockets and looked away at the picture hanging on the wall, an uninspired painting of sea and rocks and stormy skies.

'Theo, I love you. I've loved you…I feel I've loved you for ever, but there's something I have to tell you and I don't know what you're going to say. Well, actually, I can kind of guess…you're going to be angry, but I didn't feel I had a choice, just like I didn't have a choice when it came to telling you about Michael…'

'You love me. That's all that counts.' He walked towards her, prepared to fight for this amazing, vulnerable, feisty woman who had taken hold of his heart. 'If there's another man involved, then you let that go. God, Abby, I can't live without you…' He was now only inches away from her and he could see that she was shivering. He wrapped his arms around her and felt her push him away.

'Do you remember when we talked? I mean, for the last time? You told me that there was no future for us, that you could never trust me, that I could never be the sort of woman you could have a relationship with…'

'You have to forgive me for that,' Theo muttered hoarsely. He could hear the desperation in his voice and he didn't care. 'I'd never felt like this before for anyone. I didn't even recognise it for what it was. God, I was still clinging on to the belief that I could survive without you and I can't.'

Abby licked her lips nervously and looked at him. 'I

was so afraid,' she whispered. 'I knew that without love and trust, there could only be hatred if I told you…'

'Told me what?'

She squeezed her eyes shut. 'Told you that I'm expecting your baby…' She waited for the shocked reaction, for him to slam into her for deceiving him, for allowing him to walk away from his own child. It didn't come. Eventually, she opened her eyes and risked a glance at his face.

'You're…*pregnant*?'

'I thought you would hate me, would think that I had done it on purpose to try and con you into a relationship you didn't want! I thought you might try and take the baby away from me…because you didn't care about me, might see me as an unfit mother…I was afraid…'

'You're having our baby.' There was wonder in his voice and then he smiled, a slow smile that crept under her defences and sent the little seed of hope rushing upwards.

'You're not mad?'

'I'm mad because I wasted weeks, allowed you to go through all that uncertainty on your own. I'm angry with myself because…I can understand why you would have been scared of telling me after I had shut you out… God…' His voice broke and this time she crept into his arms and lost herself in him, sighing with contentment as he held her protectively into him.

'You know you'll have to marry me, don't you?'

'Theo…I understand you might just want to take it a step at a time…'

'Nothing too big, but I have a lot of family…' He looked down at her. 'There is no way I ever want to let you out of my sight again,' he said. 'I want to marry you. In fact, I'm insisting on it.' He placed one finger under her chin and kissed her gently on her mouth, tasting her like a man sipping nectar.

'In that case…yes. Yes, yes, yes!' She reached up and wrapped her arms around his neck and returned his kiss with interest. When he placed his hand on her stomach, holding it there, she felt such a swell of love and joy that she thought she might faint.

Later, much later, after he had met and charmed her mother and kept Jamie up way past his bedtime, which was fine because he still hadn't become accustomed to the rented apartment in which they were staying, he and Abby took a walk down to the beach.

She filled him in on her parents and the unexpected twist in her own life, with a mother and father who had somehow turned out to be model parents. They talked about Michael, agreeing that it was best that he was honest with himself and honest with the people he loved.

Abby felt as though she was walking on a cloud. When he seductively wondered aloud whether, as parents to be, they were too old for high jinks in the back seat of a very big car, she couldn't help but giggle.

But this time, this was very special lovemaking, exquisitely rewarding, two people touching each other in the safety of knowing that they loved and were loved in return.

The car was miles away from anywhere. 'I feel like a kid,' he groaned, pulling her to sit on him. 'It's too small, it's too uncomfortable and the windows are misting up. But, God, am I hot for you?'

'Good.' Abby opened up her shirt so that he could see the swell of her breasts and felt a heady, joyous power when he groaned.

'Your nipples are bigger and darker already.' He tested one with his tongue. 'And your breasts are heavier.' As if to prove his point, he weighed them in his hands, like ripe fruit, before returning to the job of tasting what he was holding.

'I can't wait for your belly to swell with our child,' he murmured, stroking her now. 'I've missed touching you and talking to you and waking up next to you. You are mine now and I'm never going to let you go.'

Abby sighed as he bent to suckle at her breast. Hers for ever. This wonderful, complex, loving man. Her dark, demanding, rewarding lover…

MILLS & BOON

Summer days drifting away...

Summer Loving

VICKI LEWIS THOMPSON

RHONDA NELSON

On sale 3rd June 2005

Available at most branches of WHSmith, Tesco, ASDA, Martins, Borders, Eason, Sainsbury's and all good paperback bookshops.

4 FREE

BOOKS AND A SURPRISE GIFT!

We would like to take this opportunity to thank you for reading this Mills & Boon® book by offering you the chance to take FOUR more specially selected titles from the Modern Romance™ series absolutely FREE! We're also making this offer to introduce you to the benefits of the Reader Service™—

- ★ **FREE home delivery**
- ★ **FREE gifts and competitions**
- ★ **FREE monthly Newsletter**
- ★ **Exclusive Reader Service offers**
- ★ **Books available before they're in the shops**

Accepting these FREE books and gift places you under no obligation to buy, you may cancel at any time, even after receiving your free shipment. Simply complete your details below and return the entire page to the address below. You don't even need a stamp!

YES! Please send me 4 free Modern Romance books and a surprise gift. I understand that unless you hear from me, I will receive 6 superb new titles every month for just £2.75 each, postage and packing free. I am under no obligation to purchase any books and may cancel my subscription at any time. The free books and gift will be mine to keep in any case.

P5ZED

Ms/Mrs/Miss/Mr ....Initials ....
BLOCK CAPITALS PLEASE

Surname ....

Address ....

....

....Postcode.................................

Send this whole page to:
UK: FREEPOST CN81, Croydon, CR9 3WZ